Ten Tales From
SHAKESPEARE

CHARLES AND MARY LAMB

DOVER PUBLICATIONS, INC.
Mineola, New York

EDITOR OF THIS VOLUME: JENNY BAK

Bibliographical Note

Charles and Mary Lamb's *Tales from Shakespeare* was first published in 1807. This Dover edition, first published in 2003, reprints, from a standard edition, ten of the twenty original *Tales*.

Library of Congress Cataloging-in-Publication Data

Lamb, Charles, 1775–1834.
    Ten tales from Shakespeare / Charles and Mary Lamb. [Tales from Shakespeare. Selections]
        p. cm. — (Dover evergreen classics)
    Contents: The tempest — A Midsummer night's dream — As you like it — The merchant of Venice — King Lear — Macbeth — The taming of the shrew — Romeo and Juliet — Hamlet, Prince of Denmark — Othello.
    ISBN-13: 978-0-486-42843-7 (pbk.)
    ISBN-10: 0-486-42843-5 (pbk.)
    1. Shakespeare, William, 1564–1616—Adaptations. I. Lamb, Mary, 1764–1847. II. Title. III. Series.

PR2877 .L3 2003
823'.7—dc21

                                                                    2002035174

Manufactured in the United States by Courier Corporation
42843505   2013
www.doverpublications.com

Ten Tales From Shakespeare

Contents

THE TEMPEST

There was a certain island in the sea, the only inhabitants of which were an old man, whose name was Prospero, and his daughter Miranda, a very beautiful young lady. She came to this island so young, that she had no memory of having seen any other human face than her father's.

They lived in a cave or cell, made out of a rock; it was divided into several apartments, one of which Prospero called his study; there he kept his books, which chiefly treated of magic, a study at that time much affected by all learned men: and the knowledge of this art he found very useful to him; for being thrown by a strange chance upon this island, which had been enchanted by a witch called Sycorax, who died there a short time before his arrival, Prospero, by virtue of his art, released many good spirits that Sycorax had imprisoned in the bodies of large trees, because they had refused to execute her wicked commands. These gentle spirits were ever after obedient to the will of Prospero. Of these Ariel was the chief.

The lively little sprite Ariel had nothing mischievous in his nature, except that he took rather too much pleasure in tormenting an ugly monster called Caliban, for he owed him a grudge because he was the son of his old enemy Sycorax. This Caliban, Prospero found in the woods, a strange misshapen thing, far less human in form than an ape: he took him home to his cell, and taught him to speak; and Prospero would have been very kind to him, but the bad nature which Caliban inherited from his mother

Sycorax, would not let him learn anything good or useful: therefore he was employed like a slave, to fetch wood, and do the most laborious offices; and Ariel had the charge of compelling him to these services.

When Caliban was lazy and neglected his work, Ariel (who was invisible to all eyes but Prospero's) would come slyly and pinch him, and sometimes tumble him down in the mire; and then Ariel, in the likeness of an ape, would make mouths at him. Then swiftly changing his shape, in the likeness of a hedgehog, he would lie tumbling in Caliban's way, who feared the hedgehog's sharp quills would prick his bare feet. With a variety of such-like vexatious tricks Ariel would often torment him, whenever Caliban neglected the work which Prospero commanded him to do.

Having these powerful spirits obedient to his will, Prospero could by their means command the winds, and the waves of the sea. By his orders they raised a violent storm, in the midst of which, and struggling with the wild sea-waves that every moment threatened to swallow it up, he showed his daughter a fine large ship, which he told her was full of living beings like themselves. 'O my dear father,' said she, 'if by your art you have raised this dreadful storm, have pity on their sad distress. See! the vessel will be dashed to pieces. Poor souls! they will all perish. If I had power, I would sink the sea beneath the earth, rather than the good ship should be destroyed, with all the precious souls within her.'

'Be not so amazed, daughter Miranda,' said Prospero; 'there is no harm done. I have so ordered it, that no person in the ship shall receive any hurt. What I have done has been in care of you, my dear child. You are ignorant who you are, or where you came from, and you know no more of me, but that I am your father, and live in this poor cave. Can you remember a time before you came to this cell? I think you cannot for you were not then three years of age.'

'Certainly I can, sir,' replied Miranda.

'By what?' asked Prospero; 'by any other house or person? Tell me what you can remember, my child.'

Miranda said: 'It seems to me like the recollection of a dream. But had I not once four or five women who attended upon me?'

Prospero answered: 'You had, and more. How is it that this still lives in your mind? Do you remember how you came here?'

'No, sir,' said Miranda, 'I remember nothing more.'

'Twelve years ago, Miranda,' continued Prospero, 'I was duke of Milan, and you were a princess, and my only heir. I had a younger brother, whose name was Antonio, to whom I trusted everything: and as I was fond of retirement and deep study, I commonly left the management of my state affairs to your uncle, my false brother (for so indeed he proved): I, neglecting all worldly ends, buried among my books, did dedicate my whole time to the bettering of my mind. My brother Antonio being thus in possession of my power, began to think himself the duke indeed. The opportunity I gave him of making himself popular among my subjects awakened in his bad nature a proud ambition to deprive me of my dukedom: this he soon effected with the aid of the king of Naples, a powerful prince, who was my enemy.'

'Wherefore,' said Miranda, 'did they not that hour destroy us?'

'My child,' answered her father, 'they durst not, so dear was the love that my people bore me. Antonio carried us on board a ship, and when we were some leagues out at sea, he forced us into a small boat, without either tackle, sail, or mast: there he left us, as he thought, to perish. But a kind lord of my court, one Gonzalo, who loved me, had privately placed in the boat, water, provisions, apparel, and some books which I prize above my dukedom.'

'O my father,' said Miranda, 'what a trouble must I have been to you then!'

'No, my love,' said Prospero, 'you were a little cherub that did preserve me. Your innocent smiles made me bear up against my misfortunes. Our food lasted till we landed on this desert island, since when my chief delight has been in teaching you, Miranda, and well have you profited by my instructions.'

'Heaven thank you, my dear father,' said Miranda. 'Now pray tell me, sir, your reason for raising this sea-storm?'

'Know then,' said her father, 'that by means of this storm, my enemies, the king of Naples, and my cruel brother, are cast ashore upon this island.'

Having so said, Prospero gently touched his daughter with his magic wand, and she fell fast asleep; for the spirit Ariel just then presented himself before his master, to give an account of the tempest, and how he had disposed of the ship's company, and though the spirits were always invisible to Miranda, Prospero did not choose she should hear him holding converse (as would seem to her) with the empty air.

'Well, my brave spirit,' said Prospero to Ariel, 'how have you performed your task?'

Ariel gave a lively description of the storm, and of the terrors of the mariners; and how the king's son, Ferdinand, was the first who leaped into the sea; and his father thought he saw his dear son swallowed up by the waves and lost. 'But he is safe,' said Ariel, 'in a corner of the isle, sitting with his arms folded, sadly lamenting the loss of the king, his father, whom he concludes drowned. Not a hair of his head is injured, and his princely garments, though drenched in the sea-waves, look fresher than before.'

'That's my delicate Ariel,' said Prospero. 'Bring him hither: my daughter must see this young prince. Where is the king, and my brother?'

'I left them,' answered Ariel, 'searching for Ferdinand, whom they have little hopes of finding, thinking they saw him perish. Of the ship's crew not one is missing; though each one thinks himself the only one saved: and the ship, though invisible to them, is safe in the harbour.'

'Ariel,' said Prospero, 'thy charge is faithfully performed: but there is more work yet.'

'Is there more work?' said Ariel. 'Let me remind you, master, you have promised me my liberty. I pray, remember, I have done you worthy service, told you no lies, made no mistakes, served you without grudge or grumbling.'

'How now!' said Prospero. 'You do not recollect what a torment I freed you from. Have you forgot the wicked witch Sycorax, who with age and envy was almost bent double? Where was she born? Speak; tell me.'

'Sir, in Algiers,' said Ariel.

'O was she so?' said Prospero. 'I must recount what you have been, which I find you do not remember. This bad witch, Sycorax, for her witchcrafts, too terrible to enter human hearing, was banished from Algiers, and here left by the sailors; and because you were a spirit too delicate to execute her wicked commands, she shut you up in a tree, where I found you howling. This torment, remember, I did free you from.'

'Pardon me, dear master,' said Ariel, ashamed to seem ungrateful; 'I will obey your commands.'

'Do so,' said Prospero, 'and I will set you free.' He then gave orders what further he would have him do; and away went Ariel, first to where he had left Ferdinand, and found him still sitting on the grass in the same melancholy posture.

'O my young gentleman,' said Ariel, when he saw him, 'I will soon move you. You must be brought, I find, for the Lady Miranda to have a sight of your pretty person. Come, sir, follow me.' He then began singing:

'Full fathom five thy father lies:
     Of his bones are coral made;
Those are pearls that were his eyes:
     Nothing of him that doth fade,
But doth suffer a sea-change
Into something rich and strange.
Sea-nymphs hourly ring his knell:
Hark! now I hear them,—Ding-dong, bell.'

This strange news of his lost father soon roused the prince from the stupid fit into which he had fallen. He followed in amazement the sound of Ariel's voice, till it led him to Prospero and Miranda, who were sitting under the shade of a large tree. Now Miranda had never seen a man before, except her own father.

'Miranda,' said Prospero, 'tell me what you are looking at yonder.'

'O father,' said Miranda, in a strange surprise, 'surely that is a spirit. Lord! how it looks about! Believe me, sir, it is a beautiful creature. Is it not a spirit?'

'No, girl,' answered her father; 'it eats, and sleeps, and has senses such as we have. This young man you see was in the ship. He is somewhat altered by grief, or you might call him a handsome person. He has lost his companions, and is wandering about to find them.'

Miranda, who thought all men had grave faces and grey beards like her father, was delighted with the appearance of this beautiful young prince; and Ferdinand, seeing such a lovely lady in this desert place, and from the strange sounds he had heard, expecting nothing but wonders, thought he was upon an enchanted island, and that Miranda was the goddess of the place, and as such he began to address her.

She timidly answered, she was no goddess, but a simple maid, and was going to give him an account of herself, when Prospero interrupted her. He was well pleased to find they admired each other, for he plainly perceived they had (as we say) fallen in love at first sight: but to try Ferdinand's constancy, he resolved to throw some difficulties in their way: therefore advancing forward, he addressed the prince with a stern air, telling him, he came to the island as a spy, to take it from him who was the lord of it. 'Follow me,' said he, 'I will tie you neck and feet together. You shall drink sea-water; shell-fish, withered roots, and husks of acorns shall be your food.' 'No,' said Ferdinand, 'I will resist such entertainment, till I see a more powerful enemy,' and drew his sword; but Prospero, waving his magic wand, fixed him to the spot where he stood, so that he had no power to move.

Miranda hung upon her father, saying: 'Why are you so

ungentle? Have pity, sir; I will be his surety. This is the second man I ever saw, and to me he seems a true one.'

'Silence,' said the father: 'one word more will make me chide you, girl! What! an advocate for an impostor! You think there are no more such fine men, having seen only him and Caliban. I tell you, foolish girl, most men as far excel this, as he does Caliban.' This he said to prove his daughter's constancy; and she replied: 'My affections are most humble. I have no wish to see a goodlier man.'

'Come on, young man,' said Prospero to the prince; 'you have no power to disobey me.'

'I have not indeed,' answered Ferdinand; and not knowing that it was by magic he was deprived of all power of resistance, he was astonished to find himself so strangely compelled to follow Prospero: looking back on Miranda as long as he could see her, he said, as he went after Prospero into the cave: 'My spirits are all bound up as if I were in a dream; but this man's threats, and the weakness which I feel, would seem light to me if from my prison I might once a day behold this fair maid.'

Prospero kept Ferdinand not long confined within the cell: he soon brought out his prisoner, and set him a severe task to perform, taking care to let his daughter know the hard labour he had imposed on him, and then pretending to go into his study, he secretly watched them both.

Prospero had commanded Ferdinand to pile up some heavy logs of wood. Kings' sons not being much used to laborious work, Miranda soon after found her lover almost dying with fatigue. 'Alas!' said she, 'do not work so hard; my father is at his studies, he is safe for these three hours; pray rest yourself.'

'O my dear lady,' said Ferdinand, 'I dare not. I must finish my task before I take my rest.'

'If you will sit down,' said Miranda, 'I will carry your logs the while.' But this Ferdinand would by no means agree to. Instead of a help Miranda became a hindrance, for they began a long conversation, so that the business of log-carrying went on very slowly.

Prospero, who had enjoined Ferdinand this task merely as a trial of his love, was not at his books, as his daughter supposed, but was standing by them invisible, to overhear what they said.

Ferdinand inquired her name, which she told, saying it was against her father's express command she did so.

Prospero only smiled at this first instance of his daughter's disobedience, for having by his magic art caused his daughter to fall in love so suddenly, he was not angry that she showed her love by forgetting to obey his commands. And he listened well pleased to a long speech of Ferdinand's, in which he professed to love her above all the ladies he ever saw.

In answer to his praises of her beauty, which he said exceeded all the women in the world, she replied: 'I do not remember the face of any woman, nor have I seen any more men than you, my good friend, and my dear father. How features are abroad, I know not; but, believe me, sir, I would not wish any companion in the world but you, nor can my imagination form any shape but yours that I could like. But, sir, I fear I talk to you too freely, and my father's precepts I forget.'

At this Prospero smiled, and nodded his head, as much as to say: 'This goes on exactly as I could wish; my girl will be queen of Naples.'

And then Ferdinand, in another fine long speech (for young princes speak in courtly phrases), told the innocent Miranda he was heir to the crown of Naples, and that she should be his queen.

'Ah! sir,' said she, 'I am a fool to weep at what I am glad of. I will answer you in plain and holy innocence. I am your wife if you will marry me.'

Prospero prevented Ferdinand's thanks by appearing visible before them.

'Fear nothing, my child,' said he; 'I have overheard, and approve of all you have said. And, Ferdinand, if I have too severely used you, I will make you rich amends, by giving you my daughter. All your vexations were but trials of your love, and you have nobly stood the test. Then as my gift, which your true love has worthily purchased, take my daughter, and do not smile that I boast she is above all praise.' He then, telling them that he had business which required his presence, desired they would sit down and talk together till he returned; and this command Miranda seemed not at all disposed to disobey.

When Prospero left them, he called his spirit Ariel, who quickly appeared before him, eager to relate what he had done with Prospero's brother and the king of Naples. Ariel said he had left them almost out of their senses with fear, at the strange things he had caused them to see and hear. When fatigued with wandering about, and famished for want of food, he had suddenly set before them a delicious banquet, and then, just as they were going to eat, he appeared visible before them in the shape of a harpy, a voracious monster with wings, and the feast vanished away. Then, to their utter amazement, this seeming harpy spoke to them, reminding them of their cruelty in driving Prospero from his dukedom, and leaving him and his infant daughter to perish in the sea; saying, that for this cause these terrors were suffered to afflict them.

The king of Naples, and Antonio the false brother, repented the injustice they had done to Prospero; and Ariel told his master he was certain their penitence was sincere, and that he, though a spirit, could not but pity them.

'Then bring them hither, Ariel,' said Prospero: 'if you, who are but a spirit, feel for their distress, shall not I, who am a human being like themselves, have compassion on them? Bring them, quickly, my dainty Ariel.'

Ariel soon returned with the king, Antonio, and old Gonzalo in their train, who had followed him, wondering at the wild music he played in the air to draw them on to his master's presence. This Gonzalo was the same who had so kindly provided Prospero formerly with books and provisions, when his wicked brother left him, as he thought, to perish in an open boat in the sea.

Grief and terror had so stupefied their senses, that they did not know Prospero. He first discovered himself to the good old Gonzalo, calling him the preserver of his life; and then his brother and the king knew that he was the injured Prospero.

Antonio with tears, and sad words of sorrow and true repentance, implored his brother's forgiveness, and the king expressed his sincere remorse for having assisted Antonio to depose his brother: and Prospero forgave them; and, upon their engaging to restore his dukedom, he said to the king of Naples: 'I have a gift in store for you too'; and opening a door, showed him his son Ferdinand playing at chess with Miranda.

Nothing could exceed the joy of the father and the son at this unexpected meeting, for they each thought the other drowned in the storm.

'O wonder!' said Miranda, 'what noble creatures these are! It must surely be a brave world that has such people in it.'

The king of Naples was almost as much astonished at the beauty and excellent graces of the young Miranda, as his son had been. 'Who is this maid?' said he; 'she seems the goddess that has parted us, and brought us thus together.' 'No, sir,' answered Ferdinand, smiling to find his father had fallen into the same mistake that he had done when he first saw Miranda, 'she is a mortal but by immortal Providence she is mine; I chose her when I could not ask you, my father, for your consent, not thinking you were alive. She is the daughter to this Prospero, who is the famous duke of Milan, of whose renown I have heard so much, but never saw him till now: of him I have received a new life: he has made himself to me a second father, giving me this dear lady.'

'Then I must be her father,' said the king; 'but oh! how oddly will it sound, that I must ask my child forgiveness.'

'No more of that,' said Prospero: 'let us not remember our troubles past, since they so happily have ended.' And then Prospero embraced his brother, and again assured him of his forgiveness; and said that a wise overruling Providence had permitted that he should be driven from his poor dukedom of Milan, that his daughter might inherit the crown of Naples, for that by their meeting in this desert island, it had happened that the king's son had loved Miranda.

These kind words which Prospero spoke, meaning to comfort his brother, so filled Antonio with shame and remorse, that he wept and was unable to speak; and the kind old Gonzalo wept to see this joyful reconciliation, and prayed for blessings on the young couple.

Prospero now told them that their ship was safe in the harbour, and the sailors all on board her, and that he and his daughter would accompany them home the next morning. 'In the meantime,' says he, 'partake of such refreshments as my poor cave affords; and for your evening's entertainment I will relate the history of my life from my first landing in this desert island.' He then called for Caliban to prepare some food, and set the cave in order; and the company were astonished at the uncouth form and savage appearance of this ugly monster, who (Prospero said) was the only attendant he had to wait upon him.

Before Prospero left the island, he dismissed Ariel from his service, to the great joy of that lively little spirit; who, though he had been a faithful servant to his master, was always longing to enjoy his free liberty, to wander uncontrolled in the air, like a wild bird, under green trees, among pleasant fruits, and sweet-smelling flowers. 'My quaint Ariel,' said Prospero to the little sprite when he made him free, 'I shall miss you; yet you shall have your freedom.' 'Thank you, my dear master,' said Ariel; 'but give me leave to attend your ship home with prosperous gales, before you bid farewell to the assistance of your faithful spirit; and then, master, when I am free, how merrily I shall live!' Here Ariel sung this pretty song:

'Where the bee sucks there suck I;
    In a cowslip's bell I lie;
    There I crouch when owls do cry.
    On the bat's back I do fly
    After summer merrily.
        Merrily, merrily shall I live now
    Under the blossom that hangs on the bough.'

Prospero then buried deep in the earth his magical books
and wand, for he was resolved never more to make use of
the magic art. And having thus overcome his enemies,
and being reconciled to his brother and the king of
Naples, nothing now remained to complete his happiness,
but to revisit his native land, to take possession of his
dukedom, and to witness the happy nuptials of his daughter and Prince Ferdinand, which the king said should be
instantly celebrated with great splendour on their return
to Naples. At which place, under the safe convoy of the
spirit Ariel, they, after a pleasant voyage, soon arrived.

A MIDSUMMER NIGHT'S DREAM

There was a law in the city of Athens which gave to its citizens the power of compelling their daughters to marry whomsoever they pleased; for upon a daughter's refusing to marry the man her father had chosen to be her husband, the father was empowered by this law to cause her to be put to death; but as fathers do not often desire the death of their own daughters, even though they do happen to prove a little refractory, this law was seldom or never put in execution, though perhaps the young ladies of that city were not unfrequently threatened by their parents with the terrors of it.

There was one instance, however, of an old man, whose name was Egeus, who actually did come before Theseus (at that time the reigning duke of Athens), to complain that his daughter Hermia, whom he had commanded to marry Demetrius, a young man of a noble Athenian family, refused to obey him, because she loved another young Athenian, named Lysander. Egeus demanded justice of Theseus, and desired that this cruel law might be put in force against his daughter.

Hermia pleaded in excuse for her disobedience, that Demetrius had formerly professed love for her dear friend Helena, and that Helena loved Demetrius to distraction; but this honourable reason, which Hermia gave for not obeying her father's command, moved not the stern Egeus.

Theseus, though a great and merciful prince, had no power to alter the laws of his country; therefore he could only give Hermia four days to consider of it: and at the end of that time, if she still refused to marry Demetrius, she was to be put to death.

When Hermia was dismissed from the presence of the duke, she went to her lover Lysander, and told him the peril she was in, and that she must either give him up and marry Demetrius, or lose her life in four days.

Lysander was in great affliction at hearing these evil tidings; but recollecting that he had an aunt who lived at some distance from Athens, and that at the place where she lived the cruel law could not be put in force against Hermia (this law not extending beyond the boundaries of the city), he proposed to Hermia that she should steal out of her father's house that night, and go with him to his aunt's house, where he would marry her. 'I will meet you,' said Lysander, 'in the wood a few miles without the city; in that delightful wood where we have so often walked with Helena in the pleasant month of May.'

To this proposal Hermia joyfully agreed; and she told no one of her intended flight but her friend Helena. Helena (as maidens will do foolish things for love) very ungenerously resolved to go and tell this to Demetrius, though she could hope no benefit from betraying her friend's secret, but the poor pleasure of following her faithless lover to the wood; for she well knew that Demetrius would go thither in pursuit of Hermia.

The wood in which Lysander and Hermia proposed to meet was the favourite haunt of those little beings known by the name of *Fairies*.

Oberon the king, and Titania the queen of the fairies, with all their tiny train of followers, in this wood held their midnight revels.

Between this little king and queen of sprites there happened, at this time, a sad disagreement; they never met by moonlight in the shady walks of this pleasant wood, but they were quarrelling, till all their fairy elves would creep into acorn-cups and hide themselves for fear.

The cause of this unhappy disagreement was Titania's

refusing to give Oberon a little changeling boy, whose mother had been Titania's friend; and upon her death the fairy queen stole the child from its nurse, and brought him up in the woods.

The night on which the lovers were to meet in this wood, as Titania was walking with some of her maids of honour, she met Oberon attended by his train of fairy courtiers.

'I'll met by moonlight, proud Titania,' said the fairy king. The queen replied: 'What, jealous Oberon, is it you? Fairies, skip hence; I have foresworn his company.' 'Tarry, rash fairy,' said Oberon; 'am not I thy lord? Why does Titania cross her Oberon? Give me your little changeling boy to be my page.'

'Set your heart at rest,' answered the queen; 'your whole fairy kingdom buys not the boy of me.' She then left her lord in great anger. 'Well, go your way,' said Oberon: 'before the morning dawns I will torment you for this injury.'

Oberon then sent for Puck, his chief favourite and privy counsellor.

Puck (or as he was sometimes called, Robin Goodfellow) was a shrewd and knavish sprite, that used to play comical pranks in the neighbouring villages; sometimes getting into the dairies and skimming the milk, sometimes plunging his light and airy form into the butter-churn, and while he was dancing his fantastic shape in the churn, in vain the dairymaid would labour to change her cream into butter: nor had the village swains any better success; whenever Puck chose to play his freaks in the brewing copper, the ale was sure to be spoiled. When a few good neighbours were met to drink some comfortable ale together, Puck would jump into the bowl of ale in the likeness of a roasted crab, and when some old goody was going to drink he would bob against her lips, and spill the ale over her withered chin; and presently after, when the same old dame was gravely seating herself to tell her neighbours a sad and melancholy story, Puck would slip

her three-legged stool from under her, and down toppled
the poor old woman, and then the old gossips would hold
their sides and laugh at her, and swear they never wasted
a merrier hour.

'Come hither, Puck,' said Oberon to this little merry
wanderer of the night; 'fetch me the flower which maids
call *Love in Idleness;* the juice of that little purple flower
laid on the eyelids of those who sleep, will make them,
when they awake, dote on the first thing they see. Some of
the juice of that flower I will drop on the eyelids of my
Titania when she is asleep; and the first thing she looks
upon when she opens her eyes she will fall in love with,
even though it be a lion or a bear, a meddling monkey, or
a busy ape; and before I will take this charm from off her
sight, which I can do with another charm I know of, I will
make her give me that boy to be my page.'

Puck, who loved mischief to his heart, was highly
diverted with this intended frolic of his master, and ran to
seek the flower; and while Oberon was waiting the return
of Puck, he observed Demetrius and Helena enter the
wood: he overheard Demetrius reproaching Helena for following him, and after many unkind words on his part, and
gentle expostulations from Helena, reminding him of his
former love and professions of true faith to her, he left her
(as he said) to the mercy of the wild beasts, and she ran
after him as swiftly as she could.

The fairy king, who was always friendly to true lovers,
felt great compassion for Helena; and perhaps, as
Lysander said they used to walk by moonlight in this
pleasant wood, Oberon might have seen Helena in those
happy times when she was beloved by Demetrius. However that might be, when Puck returned with the little purple flower, Oberon said to his favourite: 'Take a part of
this flower; there has been a sweet Athenian lady here,
who is in love with a disdainful youth; if you find him
sleeping, drop some of the love-juice in his eyes, but contrive to do it when she is near him, that the first thing he
sees when he awakes may be this despised lady. You will

know the man by the Athenian garments which he wears.' Puck promised to manage this matter very dexterously: and then Oberon went, unperceived by Titania, to her bower, where she was preparing to go to rest. Her fairy bower was a bank, where grew wild thyme, cowslips, and sweet violets, under a canopy of wood-bine, muskroses, and eglantine. There Titania always slept some part of the night; her coverlet the enamelled skin of a snake, which, though a small mantle, was wide enough to wrap a fairy in.

He found Titania giving orders to her fairies, how they were to employ themselves while she slept. 'Some of you,' said her majesty, 'must kill cankers in the musk-rose buds, and some wage war with the bats for their leathern wings, to make my small elves coats; and some of you keep watch that the clamorous owl, that nightly hoots, come not near me: but first sing me to sleep.' Then they began to sing this song:

> 'You spotted snakes with double tongue,
> Thorny hedgehogs, be not seen;
> Newts and blind-worms do no wrong,
> Come not near our Fairy Queen.
> Philomel, with melody,
> Sing in our sweet lullaby,
> Lulla, lulla, lullaby; lulla, lulla, lullaby;
> Never harm, nor spell, nor charm,
> Come our lovely lady nigh;
> So good night with lullaby.'

When the fairies had sung their queen asleep with this pretty lullaby, they left her to perform the important services she had enjoined them. Oberon then softly drew near his Titania, and dropped some of the love-juice on her eyelids, saying:

> 'What thou seest when thou dost wake,
> Do it for thy true-love take.'

But to return to Hermia, who made her escape out of her father's house that night, to avoid the death she was doomed to for refusing to marry Demetrius. When she entered the wood, she found her dear Lysander waiting for her, to conduct her to his aunt's house; but before they had passed half through the wood, Hermia was so much fatigued, that Lysander, who was very careful of this dear lady, who had proved her affection for him even by hazarding her life for his sake, persuaded her to rest till morning on a bank of soft moss, and lying down himself on the ground at some little distance, they soon fell fast asleep. Here they were found by Puck, who, seeing a handsome young man asleep, and perceiving that his clothes were made in the Athenian fashion, and that a pretty lady was sleeping near him, concluded that this must be the Athenian maid and her disdainful lover whom Oberon had sent him to seek; and he naturally enough conjectured that, as they were alone together, she must be the first thing he would see when he awoke; so, without more ado, he proceeded to pour some of the juice of the little purple flower into his eyes. But it so fell out, that Helena came that way, and, instead of Hermia, was the first object Lysander beheld when he opened his eyes; and strange to relate, so powerful was the love-charm, all his love for Hermia vanished away, and Lysander fell in love with Helena.

Had he first seen Hermia when he awoke, the blunder Puck committed would have been of no consequence, for he could not love that faithful lady too well; but for poor Lysander to be forced by a fairy love-charm to forget his own true Hermia, and to run after another lady, and leave Hermia asleep quite alone in a wood at midnight, was a sad chance indeed.

Thus this misfortune happened. Helena, as has been before related, endeavoured to keep pace with Demetrius when he ran away so rudely from her; but she could not continue this unequal race long, men being always better runners in a long race than ladies. Helena soon lost sight of Demetrius; and as she was wandering about, dejected and forlorn, she arrived at the place where Lysander was sleeping. 'Ah!' said she, 'this is Lysander lying on the ground: is he dead or asleep?' Then, gently touching him, she said: 'Good sir, if you are alive, awake.' Upon this Lysander opened his eyes, and (the love-charm beginning to work) immediately addressed her in terms of extravagant love and admiration; telling her she as much excelled Hermia in beauty as a dove does a raven, and that he would run through fire for her sweet sake; and many more such lover-like speeches. Helena, knowing Lysander was her friend Hermia's lover, and that he was solemnly engaged to marry her, was in the utmost rage when she heard herself addressed in this manner; for she thought (as well she might) that Lysander was making a jest of her. 'Oh!' said she, 'why was I born to be mocked and scorned by every one? Is it not enough, is it not enough, young man, that I can never get a sweet look or a kind word from Demetrius; but you, sir, must pretend in this disdainful manner to court me? I thought, Lysander, you were a lord of more true gentleness.' Saying these words in great anger, she ran away; and Lysander followed her, quite forgetful of his own Hermia, who was still asleep.

When Hermia awoke, she was in a sad fright at finding herself alone. She wandered about the wood, not knowing what was become of Lysander, or which way to go to seek for him. In the meantime Demetrius, not being able to find Hermia and his rival Lysander, and fatigued with his fruitless search, was observed by Oberon fast asleep. Oberon had learnt by some questions he had asked of Puck, that he had applied the love-charm to the wrong person's eyes; and now having found the person first intended, he touched the eyelids of the sleeping Demetrius with the love-juice, and he instantly awoke; and the first thing he saw being Helena, he, as Lysander had done before, began to address love-speeches to her; and just at that moment Lysander, followed by Hermia (for through Puck's unlucky mistake it was now become Hermia's turn to run after her lover) made his appearance; and then Lysander and Demetrius, both speaking together, made love to Helena, they being each one under the influence of the same potent charm.

The astonished Helena thought that Demetrius, Lysander, and her once dear friend Hermia, were all in a plot together to make a jest of her.

Hermia was as much surprised as Helena; she knew not why Lysander and Demetrius, who both before loved her, were now become the lovers of Helena; and to Hermia the matter seemed to be no jest.

The ladies, who before had always been the dearest of friends, now fell to high words together.

'Unkind Hermia,' said Helena, 'it is you have set Lysander on to vex me with mock praises; and your other lover Demetrius, who used almost to spurn me with his foot, have you not bid him call me Goddess, Nymph, rare, precious, and celestial? He would not speak thus to me, whom he hates, if you did not set him on to make a jest of me. Unkind Hermia, to join with men in scorning your poor friend. Have you forgot our school-day friendship? How often, Hermia, have we two, sitting on one cushion, both singing one song, with our needles working the same flower, both on the same sampler wrought; growing up together in fashion of a double cherry, scarcely seeming parted! Hermia, it is not friendly in you, it is not maidenly to join with men in scorning your poor friend.'

I am amazed at your passionate words,' said Hermia: 'I scorn you not; it seems you scorn me.' 'Ay, do,' returned Helena, 'persevere, counterfeit serious looks, and make mouths at me when I turn my back; then wink at each other, and hold the sweet jest up. If you had any pity, grace, or manners, you would not use me thus.'

While Helena and Hermia were speaking these angry words to each other, Demetrius and Lysander left them, to fight together in the wood for the love of Helena.

When they found the gentlemen had left them, they departed, and once more wandered weary in the wood in search of their lovers.

As soon as they were gone, the fairy king, who with little Puck had been listening to their quarrels, said to him: 'This is your negligence, Puck; or did you do this wilfully?' 'Believe me, king of shadows,' answered Puck, 'it was a mistake; did not you tell me I should know the man by his Athenian garments? However, I am not sorry this has happened, for I think their jangling makes excellent sport.' 'You heard,' said Oberon, 'that Demetrius and Lysander are gone to seek a convenient place to fight in. I command you to overhang the night with a thick fog, and lead these quarrelsome lovers so astray in the dark, that they shall not be able to find each other. Counterfeit each of their voices to the other, and with bitter taunts provoke them to follow you, while they think it is their rival's tongue they hear. See you do this, till they are so weary they can go no farther; and when you find they are asleep, drop the juice of this other flower into Lysander's eyes, and when he awakes he will forget his new love for Helena, and return to his old passion for Hermia; and then the two fair ladies may each one be happy with the man she loves, and they will think all that has passed a vexatious dream. About this quickly, Puck, and I will go and see what sweet love my Titania has found.'

Titania was still sleeping, and Oberon seeing a clown near her, who had lost his way in the wood, and was likewise asleep: 'This fellow,' said he, 'shall be my Titania's true love'; and clapping an ass's head over the clown's, it seemed to fit him as well as if it had grown upon his own shoulders. Though Oberon fixed the ass's head on very gently, it awakened him, and rising up, unconscious of what Oberon had done to him, he went towards the bower where the fairy queen slept.

'Ah! what angel is that I see?' said Titania, opening her eyes, and the juice of the little purple flower beginning to take effect: 'are you as wise as you are beautiful?'

'Why, mistress,' said the foolish clown, 'if I have wit enough to find the way out of this wood, I have enough to serve my turn.'

'Out of the wood do not desire to go,' said the enamoured queen. 'I am a spirit of no common rate. I love you. Go with me, and I will give you fairies to attend upon you.'

She then called four of her fairies: their names were, Pease-blossom, Cobweb, Moth, and Mustard-seed.

'Attend,' said the queen, 'upon this sweet gentleman; hop in his walks, and gambol in his sight; feed him with grapes and apricots, and steal for him the honey-bags from the bees. Come, sit with me,' said she to the clown, 'and let me play with your amiable hairy cheeks, my beautiful ass! and kiss your fair large ears, my gentle joy!'

'Where is Pease-blossom?' said the ass-headed clown, not much regarding the fairy queen's courtship, but very proud of his new attendants.

'Here, sir,' said little Pease-blossom.

'Scratch my head,' said the clown. 'Where is Cobweb?'

'Here, sir,' said Cobweb.

'Good Mr. Cobweb,' said the foolish clown, 'kill me the red humble bee on the top of that thistle yonder; and, good Mr. Cobweb, bring me the honey-bag. Do not fret yourself too much in the action, Mr. Cobweb, and take care the honey-bag break not; I should be sorry to have you overflown with a honey-bag. Where is Mustard-seed?'

'Here, sir,' said Mustard-seed: 'what is your will?'

'Nothing,' said the clown, 'good Mr. Mustard-seed, but to help Mr. Pease-blossom to scratch; I must go to a barber's, Mr. Mustard-seed, for methinks I am marvellous hairy about the face.'

'My sweet love,' said the queen, 'what will you have to eat? I have a venturous fairy shall seek the squirrel's hoard, and fetch you some new nuts.'

'I had rather have a handful of dried pease,' said the clown, who with his ass's head had got an ass's appetite. 'But, I pray, let none of your people disturb me, for I have a mind to sleep.'

'Sleep, then,' said the queen, 'and I will wind you in my arms. O how I love you! how I dote upon you!'

When the fairy king saw the clown sleeping in the arms of his queen, he advanced within her sight, and reproached her with having lavished her favours upon an ass.

This she could not deny, as the clown was then sleeping within her arms, with his ass's head crowned by her with flowers.

When Oberon had teased her for some time, he again demanded the changeling boy; which she, ashamed of being discovered by her lord with her new favourite, did not dare to refuse him.

Oberon, having thus obtained the little boy he had so long wished for to be his page, took pity on the disgraceful situation into which, by his merry contrivance, he had brought his Titania and threw some of the juice of the other flower into her eyes; and the fairy queen immediately recovered her senses, and wondered at her late dotage, saying how she now loathed the sight of the strange monster.

Oberon likewise took the ass's head from off the clown, and left him to finish his nap with his own fool's head upon his shoulders.

Oberon and his Titania being now perfectly reconciled, he related to her the history of the lovers, and their midnight quarrels; and she agreed to go with him and see the end of their adventures.

The fairy king and queen found the lovers and their fair ladies, at no great distance from each other, sleeping on a grass-plot; for Puck, to make amends for his former mistake, had contrived with the utmost diligence to bring them all to the same spot, unknown to each other: and he had carefully removed the charm from off the eyes of Lysander with the antidote the fairy king gave to him.

Hermia first awoke, and finding her lost Lysander asleep so near her, was looking at him and wondering at his strange inconstancy. Lysander presently opening his eyes, and seeing his dear Hermia, recovered his reason which the fairy charm had before clouded, and with his reason, his love for Hermia; and they began to talk over the adventures of the night, doubting if these things had really happened, or if they had both been dreaming the same bewildering dream.

Helena and Demetrius were by this time awake; and a sweet sleep having quieted Helena's disturbed and angry spirits, she listened with delight to the professions of love which Demetrius still made to her, and which, to her surprise as well as pleasure, she began to perceive were sincere.

These fair night-wandering ladies, now no longer rivals, became once more true friends; all the unkind words which had passed were forgiven, and they calmly consulted together what was best to be done in their present situation. It was soon agreed that, as Demetrius had given up his pretensions to Hermia, he should endeavour to prevail upon her father to revoke the cruel sentence of death which had been passed against her. Demetrius was preparing to return to Athens for this friendly purpose, when they were surprised with the sight of Egeus, Hermia's father, who came to the wood in pursuit of his runaway daughter.

When Egeus understood that Demetrius would not now marry his daughter, he no longer opposed her marriage with Lysander, but gave his consent that they should be wedded on the fourth day from that time, being the same day on which Hermia had been condemned to lose her life; and on that same day Helena joyfully agreed to marry her beloved and now faithful Demetrius.

The fairy king and queen, who were invisible spectators of this reconciliation, and now saw the happy ending of the lovers' history, brought about through the good offices of Oberon, received so much pleasure, that these kind spirits resolved to celebrate the approaching nuptials with sports and revels throughout their fairy kingdom.

And now, if any are offended with this story of fairies and their pranks, as judging it incredible and strange, they have only to think that they have been asleep and dreaming, and that all these adventures were visions which they saw in their sleep: and I hope none of my readers will be so unreasonable as to be offended with a pretty harmless Midsummer Night's Dream.

AS YOU LIKE IT

During the time that France was divided into provinces (or dukedoms as they were called) there reigned in one of these provinces an usurper, who had deposed and banished his elder brother, the lawful duke.

The duke, who was thus driven from his dominions, retired with a few faithful followers to the forest of Arden; and here the good duke lived with his loving friends, who had put themselves into a voluntary exile for his sake, while their land and revenues enriched the false usurper; and custom soon made the life of careless ease they led here more sweet to them than the pomp and uneasy splendour of a courtier's life. Here they lived like the old Robin Hood of England, and to this forest many noble youths daily resorted from the court, and did fleet the time carelessly, as they did who lived in the golden age. In the summer they lay along under the fine shade of the large forest trees, marking the playful sports of the wild deer; and so fond were they of these poor dappled fools, who seemed to be the native inhabitants of the forest, that it grieved them to be forced to kill them to supply themselves with venison for their food. When the cold winds of winter made the duke feel the change of his adverse fortune, he would endure it patiently, and say: 'These chilling winds which blow upon my body are true counsellors; they do not flatter, but represent truly to me my condition; and though they bite sharply, their tooth is nothing like so keen as that of unkindness and ingratitude.

I find that howsoever men speak against adversity, yet some sweet uses are to be extracted from it; like the jewel, precious for medicine, which is taken from the head of the venomous and despised toad.' In this manner did the patient duke draw a useful moral from everything that he saw; and by the help of this moralizing turn, in that life of his, remote from public haunts, he could find tongues in trees, books in the running brooks, sermons in stones, and good in everything.

The banished duke had an only daughter, named Rosalind, whom the usurper, duke Frederick, when he banished her father, still retained in his court as a companion for his own daughter Celia. A strict friendship subsisted between these ladies, which the disagreement between their fathers did not in the least interrupt, Celia striving by every kindness in her power to make amends to Rosalind for the injustice of her own father in deposing the father of Rosalind; and whenever the thoughts of her father's banishment, and her own dependence on the false usurper, made Rosalind melancholy, Celia's whole care was to comfort and console her.

One day, when Celia was talking in her usual kind manner to Rosalind, saying: 'I pray you, Rosalind, my sweet cousin, be merry,' a messenger entered from the duke, to tell them that if they wished to see a wrestling match, which was just going to begin, they must come instantly to the court before the palace; and Celia, thinking it would amuse Rosalind, agreed to go and see it.

In those times wrestling, which is only practised now by country clowns, was a favourite sport even in the courts of princes, and before fair ladies and princesses. To this wrestling match, therefore, Celia and Rosalind went. They found that it was likely to prove a very tragical sight; for a large and powerful man, who had been long practised in the art of wrestling, and had slain many men in contests of this kind, was just going to wrestle with a very young man, who, from his extreme youth and inexperience in the art, the beholders all thought would certainly be killed.

When the duke saw Celia and Rosalind, he said: 'How now, daughter and niece, are you crept hither to see the wrestling? You will take little delight in it, there is such odds in the men: in pity to this young man, I would wish to persuade him from wrestling. Speak to him, ladies, and see if you can move him.'

The ladies were well pleased to perform this humane office, and first Celia entreated the young stranger that he would desist from the attempt; and then Rosalind spoke so kindly to him, and with such feeling consideration for, the danger he was about to undergo, that instead of being persuaded by her gentle words to forgo his purpose, all his thoughts were bent to distinguish himself by his courage in this lovely lady's eyes. He refused the request of Celia and Rosalind in such graceful and modest words, that they felt still more concern for him; he concluded his refusal with saying: 'I am sorry to deny such fair and excellent ladies anything. But let your fair eyes and gentle wishes go with me to my trial, wherein if I be conquered there is one shamed that was never gracious; if I am killed, there is one dead that is willing to die; I shall do my friends no wrong, for I have none to lament me; the world no injury, for in it I have nothing; for I only fill up a place in the world which may be better supplied when I have made it empty.'

And now the wrestling match began. Celia wished the young stranger might not be hurt; but Rosalind felt most for him. The friendless state which he said he was in, and that he wished to die, made Rosalind think that he was like herself, unfortunate; and she pitied him so much, and so deep an interest she took in his danger while he was wrestling, that she might almost be said at that moment to have fallen in love with him.

The kindness shown this unknown youth by these fair and noble ladies gave him courage and strength, so that he performed wonders; and in the end completely conquered his antagonist, who was so much hurt, that for a while he was unable to speak or move.

The duke Frederick was much pleased with the courage and skill shown by this young stranger; and desired to know his name and parentage, meaning to take him under his protection.

The stranger said his name was Orlando, and that he was the youngest son of Sir Roland de Boys.

Sir Rowland de Boys, the father of Orlando, had been dead some years; but when he was living, he had been a true subject and dear friend of the banished duke; therefore, when Frederick heard Orlando was the son of his banished brother's friend, all his liking for this brave young man was changed into displeasure, and he left the place in very ill humour. Hating to hear the very name of any of his brother's friends, and yet still admiring the valour of the youth, he said, as he went out, that he wished Orlando had been the son of any other man.

Rosalind was delighted to hear that her new favourite was the son of her father's old friend; and she said to Celia: 'My father loved Sir Rowland de Boys, and if I had known this young man was his son, I would have added tears to my entreaties before he should have ventured.'

The ladies then went up to him; and seeing him abashed by the sudden displeasure shown by the duke, they spoke kind and encouraging words to him; and Rosalind, when they were going away, turned back to speak some more civil things to the brave young son of her father's old friend; and taking a chain from off her neck, she said: 'Gentleman, wear this for me. I am out of suits with fortune, or I would give you a more valuable present.'

When the ladies were alone, Rosalind's talk being still of Orlando, Celia began to perceive her cousin had fallen in love with the handsome young wrestler, and she said to Rosalind: 'Is it possible you should fall in love so suddenly?' Rosalind replied: 'The duke, my father, loved his father dearly.' 'But,' said Celia, 'does it therefore follow that you should love his son dearly? for then I ought to hate him, for my father hated his father; yet I do not hate Orlando.'

Frederick being enraged at the sight of Sir Rowland de Boys' son, which reminded him of the many friends the banished duke had among the nobility, and having been for some time displeased with his niece, because the people praised her for her virtues, and pitied her for her good father's sake, his malice suddenly broke out against her; and while Celia and Rosalind were talking of Orlando, Frederick entered the room, and with looks full of anger ordered Rosalind instantly to leave the palace, and follow her father into banishment; telling Celia, who in vain pleaded for her, that he had only suffered Rosalind to stay upon her account. 'I did not then,' said Celia, 'entreat you to let her stay, for I was too young at that time to value her; but now that I know her worth, and that we so long have slept together, rose at the same instant, learned, played, and eat together, I cannot live out of her company.' Frederick replied: 'She is too subtle for you; her smoothness, her very silence, and her patience speak to the people, and they pity her. You are a fool to plead for her, for you will seem more bright and virtuous when she is gone; therefore open not your lips in her favour, for the doom which I have passed upon her is irrevocable.'

When Celia found she could not prevail upon her father to let Rosalind remain with her, she generously resolved to accompany her; and leaving her father's palace that night, she went along with her friend to seek Rosalind's father, the banished duke, in the forest of Arden.

Before they set out, Celia considered that it would be unsafe for two young ladies to travel in the rich clothes they then wore; she therefore proposed that they should disguise their rank by dressing themselves like country maids. Rosalind said it would be a still greater protection if one of them was to be dressed like a man; and so it was quickly agreed on between them, that as Rosalind was the tallest, she should wear the dress of a young countryman, and Celia should be habited like a country lass, and that they should say they were brother and sister, and Rosalind said she would be called Ganymede, and Celia chose the name of Aliena.

In this disguise, and taking their money and jewels to defray their expenses, these fair princesses set out on their long travel; for the forest of Arden was a long way off, beyond the boundaries of the duke's dominions.

The Lady Rosalind (or Ganymede as she must now be called) with her manly garb seemed to have put on a manly courage. The faithful friendship Celia had shown in accompanying Rosalind so many weary miles, made the new brother, in recompense for this true love, exert a cheerful spirit, as if he were indeed Ganymede, the rustic and stout-hearted brother of the gentle village maiden, Aliena.

When at last they came to the forest of Arden, they no longer found the convenient inns and good accommodations they had met with on the road; and being in want of food and rest, Ganymede, who had so merrily cheered his sister with pleasant speeches and happy remarks all the way, now owned to Aliena that he was so weary, he could find in his heart to disgrace his man's apparel, and cry like a woman; and Aliena declared she could go no farther; and then again Ganymede tried to recollect that it was a man's duty to comfort and console a woman, as the weaker vessel; and to seem courageous to his new sister; he said: 'Come, have a good heart, my sister Aliena; we are now at the end of our travel, in the forest of Arden.' But feigned manliness and forced courage would no longer support them; for though they were in the forest of Arden, they knew not where to find the duke: and here the travel of these weary ladies might have come to a sad conclusion, for they might have lost themselves, and perished for want of food; but providentially, as they were sitting on the grass, almost dying with fatigue and hopeless of any relief, a countryman chanced to pass that way, and Ganymede once more tried to speak with a manly boldness, saying: 'Shepherd, if love or gold can in this desert place procure us entertainment, I pray you bring us where we may rest ourselves; for this young maid, my sister, is much fatigued with travelling, and faints for want of food.'

The man replied that he was only a servant to a shepherd, and that his master's house was just going to be sold, and therefore they would find but poor entertainment; but that if they would go with him, they should be welcome to what there was. They followed the man, the near prospect of relief giving them fresh strength; and bought the house and sheep of the shepherd, and took the man who conducted them to the shepherd's house to wait on them; and being by this means so fortunately provided with a neat cottage, and well supplied with provisions, they agreed to stay here till they could learn in what part of the forest the duke dwelt.

When they were rested after the fatigue of their journey, they began to like their new way of life, and almost fancied themselves the shepherd and shepherdess they feigned to be: yet sometimes Ganymede remembered he had once been the same Lady Rosalind who had so dearly loved the brave Orlando, because he was the son of old Sir Rowland, her father's friend; and though Ganymede thought that Orlando was many miles distant, even so many weary miles as they had travelled, yet it soon appeared that Orlando was also in the forest of Arden: and in this manner this strange event came to pass.

Orlando was the youngest son of Sir Rowland de Boys, who, when he died, left him (Orlando being then very young) to the care of his eldest brother Oliver, charging Oliver on his blessing to give his brother a good education, and provide for him as became the dignity of their ancient house. Oliver proved an unworthy brother; and disregarding the commands of his dying father, he never put his brother to school, but kept him at home untaught and entirely neglected. But in his nature and in the noble qualities of his mind Orlando so much resembled his excellent father, that without any advantages of education he seemed like a youth who had been bred with the utmost care; and Oliver so envied the fine person and dignified manners of his untutored brother, that at last he wished to destroy him; and to effect this he set on people to persuade him to wrestle with the famous wrestler, who, as has been before related, had killed so many men. Now,

it was this cruel brother's neglect of him which made
Orlando say he wished to die, being so friendless.

When, contrary to the wicked hopes he had formed, his
brother proved victorious, his envy and malice knew no
bounds, and he swore he would burn the chamber where
Orlando slept. He was overheard making this vow by one
that had been an old and faithful servant to their father,
and that loved Orlando because he resembled Sir Rowland.
This old man went out to meet him when he returned
from the duke's palace, and when he saw Orlando, the
peril his dear young master was in made him break out
into these passionate exclamations: 'O my gentle master,
my sweet master, O you memory of old Sir Rowland! why
are you virtuous? why are you gentle, strong, and valiant?
and why would you be so fond to overcome the famous
wrestler? Your praise is come too swiftly home before
you.' Orlando, wondering what all this meant, asked him
what was the matter. And then the old man told him how
his wicked brother, envying the love all people bore him,
and now hearing the fame he had gained by his victory in
the duke's palace, intended to destroy him, by setting fire
to his chamber that night; and in conclusion, advised him
to escape the danger he was in by instant flight; and
knowing Orlando had no money, Adam (for that was the
good old man's name) had brought out with him his own
little hoard, and he said: 'I have five hundred crowns, the
thrifty hire I saved under your father, and laid by to be
provision for me when my old limbs should become unfit
for service; take that, and He that doth the ravens feed be
comfort to my age! Here is the gold; all this I give to you:
let me be your servant; though I look old I will do the service of a younger man in all your business and necessi-
ties.' 'O good old man!' said Orlando, 'how well appears in
you the constant service of the old world! You are not for
the fashion of these times. We will go along together, and
before your youthful wages are spent, I shall light upon
some means for both our maintenance.'

Together then this faithful servant and his loved master

set out; and Orlando and Adam travelled on, uncertain what course to pursue, till they came to the forest of Arden, and there they found themselves in the same distress for want of food that Ganymede and Aliena had been. They wandered on, seeking some human habitation, till they were almost spent with hunger and fatigue. Adam at last said: 'O my dear master, I die for want of food, I can go no farther!' He then laid himself down, thinking to make that place his grave, and bade his dear master farewell. Orlando, seeing him in this weak state, took his old servant up in his arms, and carried him under the shelter of some pleasant trees; and he said to him: 'Cheerly, old Adam, rest your weary limbs here awhile, and do not talk of dying!'

Orlando then searched about to find some food, and he happened to arrive at that part of the forest where the duke was; and he and his friends were just going to eat their dinner, this royal duke being seated on the grass, under no other canopy than the shady covert of some large trees.

Orlando, whom hunger had made desperate, drew his sword, intending to take their meat by force, and said: 'Forbear and eat no more; I must have your food!' The duke asked him, if distress had made him so bold, or if he were a rude despiser of good manners? On this Orlando said, he was dying with hunger; and then the duke told him he was welcome to sit down and eat with them. Orlando hearing him speak so gently, put up his sword, and blushed with shame at the rude manner in which he had demanded their food. 'Pardon me, I pray you,' said he: 'I thought that all things had been savage here, and therefore I put on the countenance of stern command; but whatever men you are, that in this desert, under the shade of melancholy boughs, lose and neglect the creeping hours of time; if ever you have looked on better days; if ever you have been where bells have knolled to church; if you have ever sat at any good man's feast; if ever from your eyelids you have wiped a tear, and know what it is to pity or be pitied, may gentle speeches now move you to do me human courtesy!' The duke replied: 'True it is that we are men (as you say) who have seen better days, and though we have now our habitation in this wild forest, we have lived in towns and cities, and have with holy bell been knolled to church, have sat at good men's feasts, and from our eyes have wiped the drops which sacred pity has engendered; therefore sit you down, and take of our refreshment as much as will minister to your wants.' 'There is an old poor man,' answered Orlando, 'who has limped after me many a weary step in pure love, oppressed at once with two sad infirmities, age and hunger; till he be satisfied, I must not touch a bit.' 'Go, find him out, and bring him hither,' said the duke; 'we will forbear to eat till you return.' Then Orlando went like a doe to find its fawn and give it food; and presently returned, bringing Adam in his arms; and the duke said: 'Set down your venerable burthen; you are both welcome'; and they fed the old man, and cheered his heart, and he revived, and recovered his health and strength again.

The duke inquired who Orlando was; and when he found that he was the son of his old friend, Sir Rowland de Boys, he took him under his protection, and Orlando and his old servant lived with the duke in the forest.

Orlando arrived in the forest not many days after Ganymede and Aliena came there, and (as has been before related) bought the shepherd's cottage.

Ganymede and Aliena were strangely surprised to find the name of Rosalind carved on the trees, and love-sonnets, fastened to them, all addressed to Rosalind; and while they were wondering how this could be, they met Orlando, and they perceived the chain which Rosalind had given him about his neck.

Orlando little thought that Ganymede was the fair princess Rosalind, who, by her noble condescension and favour, had so won his heart that he passed his whole time in carving her name upon the trees, and writing sonnets in praise of her beauty: but being much pleased with the graceful air of this pretty shepherd-youth, he entered into conversation with him, and he thought he saw a likeness in Ganymede to his beloved Rosalind, but that he had none of the dignified deportment of that noble lady; for Ganymede assumed the forward manners often seen in youths when they are between boys and men, and with much archness and humour talked to Orlando of a certain lover, 'who,' said he, 'haunts our forest, and spoils our young trees with carving Rosalind upon their barks; and he hangs odes upon hawthorns, and elegies on brambles, all praising this same Rosalind. If I could find this lover, I would give him some good counsel that would soon cure him of his love.'

Orlando confessed that he was the fond lover of whom he spoke, and asked Ganymede to give him the good counsel he talked of. The remedy Ganymede proposed, and the counsel he gave him, was that Orlando should come every day to the cottage where he and his sister Aliena dwelt: 'And then,' said Ganymede, 'I will feign myself to be Rosalind, and you shall feign to court me in the same manner as you would do if I was Rosalind, and then I will imitate the fantastic ways of whimsical ladies to their lovers, till I make you ashamed of your love; and this is the way I propose to cure you.' Orlando had no great faith in the remedy, yet he agreed to come every day to Ganymede's cottage, and feign a playful courtship; and every day Orlando visited Ganymede and Aliena, and Orlando called the shepherd Ganymede his Rosalind, and every day talked over all the fine words and flattering compliments which young men delight to use when they court their mistresses. It does not appear, however, that Ganymede made any progress in curing Orlando of his love for Rosalind.

Though Orlando thought all this was but a sportive play (not dreaming that Ganymede was his very Rosalind), yet the opportunity it gave him of saying all the fond things he had in his heart, pleased his fancy almost as well as it did Ganymede's, who enjoyed the secret jest in knowing these fine love-speeches were all addressed to the right person.

In this manner many days passed pleasantly on with these young people; and the good-natured Aliena, seeing it made Ganymede happy, let him have his own way, and was diverted at the mock-courtship, and did not care to remind Ganymede that the Lady Rosalind had not yet made herself known to the duke her father, whose place of resort in the forest they had learnt from Orlando. Ganymede met the duke one day, and had some talk with him, and the duke asked of what parentage he came. Ganymede answered that he came of as good parentage as he did, which made the duke smile, for he did not suspect the pretty shepherd-boy came of royal lineage. Then seeing the duke look well and happy, Ganymede was content to put off all further explanation for a few days longer.

One morning, as Orlando was going to visit Ganymede, he saw a man lying asleep on the ground, and a large green snake had twisted itself about his neck. The snake, seeing Orlando approach, glided away among the bushes. Orlando went nearer, and then he discovered a lioness lie crouching, with her head on the ground, with a cat-like watch, waiting until the sleeping man awaked (for it is said that lions will prey on nothing that is dead or sleeping). It seemed as if Orlando was sent by Providence to free the man from the danger of the snake and lioness; but when Orlando looked in the man's face, he perceived that the sleeper who was exposed to this double peril, was his own brother Oliver, who had so cruelly used him, and had threatened to destroy him by fire; and he was almost tempted to leave him a prey to the hungry lioness; but brotherly affection and the gentleness of his nature soon overcame his first anger against his brother; and he drew his sword, and attacked the lioness, and slew her, and thus preserved his brother's life both from the venomous snake and from the furious lioness; but before Orlando could conquer the lioness, she had torn one of his arms with her sharp claws.

While Orlando was engaged with the lioness, Oliver awaked, and perceiving that his brother Orlando, whom he had so cruelly treated, was saving him from the fury of a wild beast at the risk of his own life, shame and remorse at once seized him, and he repented of his unworthy conduct, and besought with many tears his brother's pardon for the injuries he had done him. Orlando rejoiced to see him so penitent, and readily forgave him: they embraced each other; and from that hour Oliver loved Orlando with a true brotherly affection, though he had come to the forest bent on his destruction.

The wound in Orlando's arm having bled very much, he found himself too weak to go to visit Ganymede, and therefore he desired his brother to go and tell Ganymede, 'whom,' said Orlando, 'I in sport do call my Rosalind,' the accident which had befallen him.

Thither then Oliver went, and told to Ganymede and Aliena how Orlando had saved his life: and when he had finished the story of Orlando's bravery, and his own providential escape, he owned to them that he was Orlando's brother, who had so cruelly used him; and then he told them of their reconciliation.

The sincere sorrow that Oliver expressed for his offences made such a lively impression on the kind heart of Aliena, that she instantly fell in love with him; and Oliver observing how much she pitied the distress he told her he felt for his fault, he as suddenly fell in love with her. But while love was thus stealing into the hearts of Aliena and Oliver, he was no less busy with Ganymede, who hearing of the danger Orlando had been in, and that he was wounded by the lioness, fainted; and when he recovered, he pretended that he had counterfeited the swoon in the imaginary character of Rosalind, and Ganymede said to Oliver: 'Tell your brother Orlando how well I counterfeited a swoon.' But Oliver saw by the paleness of his complexion that he did really faint, and much wondering at the weakness of the young man, he said: 'Well, if you did counterfeit, take a good heart, and counterfeit to be a man.' 'So I do,' replied Ganymede, truly, 'but I should have been a woman by right.'

Oliver made this visit a very long one, and when at last he returned back to his brother, he had much news to tell him; for besides the account of Ganymede's fainting at the hearing that Orlando was wounded, Oliver told him how he had fallen in love with the fair shepherdess Aliena, and that she had lent a favourable ear to his suit, even in this their first interview; and he talked to his brother, as of a thing almost settled, that he should marry Aliena, saying, that he so well loved her, that he would live here as a shepherd, and settle his estate and house at home upon Orlando.

'You have my consent,' said Orlando. 'Let your wedding be to-morrow, and I will invite the duke and his friends. Go and persuade your shepherdess to this: she is now alone; for look, here comes her brother.' Oliver went to Aliena; and Ganymede, whom Orlando had perceived approaching, came to inquire after the health of his wounded friend.

When Orlando and Ganymede began to talk over the sudden love which had taken place between Oliver and Aliena, Orlando said he had advised his brother to persuade his fair shepherdess to be married on the morrow, and then he added how much he could wish to be married on the same day to his Rosalind.

Ganymede, who well approved of this arrangement, said that if Orlando really loved Rosalind as well as he professed to do, he should have his wish; for on the morrow he would engage to make Rosalind appear in her own person, and also that Rosalind should be willing to marry Orlando.

This seemingly wonderful event, which, as Ganymede was the Lady Rosalind, he could so easily perform, he pretended he would bring to pass by the aid of magic, which he said he had learnt of an uncle who was a famous magician.

The fond lover Orlando, half believing and half doubting what he heard, asked Ganymede if he spoke in sober meaning. 'By my life I do,' said Ganymede; 'therefore put on your best clothes, and bid the duke and your friends to your wedding; for if you desire to be married to-morrow to Rosalind, she shall be here.'

The next morning, Oliver having obtained the consent of Aliena, they came into the presence of the duke, and with them also came Orlando.

They being all assembled to celebrate this double marriage, and as yet only one of the brides appearing, there was much of wondering and conjecture, but they mostly thought that Ganymede was making a jest of Orlando.

The duke, hearing that it was his own daughter that was to be brought in this strange way, asked Orlando if he believed the shepherd-boy could really do what he had promised; and while Orlando was answering that he knew not what to think, Ganymede entered, and asked the duke, if he brought his daughter, whether he would consent to her marriage with Orlando. 'That I would,' said the duke, 'if I had kingdoms to give with her.' Ganymede then said to Orlando: 'And you say you will marry her if I bring her here.' 'That I would,' said Orlando, 'if I were king of many kingdoms.'

Ganymede and Aliena then went out together, and Ganymede throwing off his male attire, and being once more dressed in woman's apparel, quickly became Rosalind without the power of magic; and Aliena changing her country garb for her own rich clothes, was with as little trouble transformed into the Lady Celia.

While they were gone, the duke said to Orlando, that he thought the shepherd Ganymede very like his daughter Rosalind; and Orlando said, he also had observed the resemblance.

They had no time to wonder how all this would end, for Rosalind and Celia in their own clothes entered; and no longer pretending that it was by the power of magic that she came there, Rosalind threw herself on her knees before her father, and begged his blessing. It seemed so wonderful to all present that she should so suddenly appear, that it might well have passed for magic; but

Rosalind would no longer trifle with her father, and told him the story of her banishment, and of her dwelling in the forest as a shepherd-boy, her cousin Celia passing as her sister.

The duke ratified the consent he had already given to the marriage; and Orlando and Rosalind, Oliver and Celia, were married at the same time. And though their wedding could not be celebrated in this wild forest with any of the parade or splendour usual on such occasions, yet a happier wedding-day was never passed: and while they were eating their venison under the cool shade of the pleasant trees, as if nothing should be wanting to complete the felicity of this good duke and the true lovers, an unexpected messenger arrived to tell the duke the joyful news, that his dukedom was restored to him.

The usurper, enraged at the flight of his daughter Celia, and hearing that every day men of great worth resorted to the forest of Arden to join the lawful duke in his exile, much envying that his brother should be so highly respected in his adversity, put himself at the head of a large force, and advanced towards the forest, intending to seize his brother, and put him with all his faithful followers to the sword; but, by a wonderful interposition of Providence, this bad brother was converted from his evil intention; for just as he entered the skirts of the wild forest, he was met by an old religious man, a hermit, with whom he had much talk, and who in the end completely turned his heart from his wicked design. Thenceforward he became a true penitent, and resolved, relinquishing his unjust dominion, to spend the remainder of his days in a religious house. The first act of his newly conceived penitence was to send a messenger to his brother (as has been related) to offer to restore to him his dukedom, which he had usurped so long, and with it the lands and revenues of his friends, the faithful followers of his adversity.

This joyful news, as unexpected as it was welcome, came opportunely to heighten the festivity and rejoicings at the wedding of the princesses. Celia complimented her cousin on this good fortune which had happened to the duke, Rosalind's father, and wished her joy very sincerely, though she herself was no longer heir to the dukedom, but by this restoration which her father had made, Rosalind was now the heir: so completely was the love of these two cousins unmixed with anything of jealousy or of envy.

The duke had now an opportunity of rewarding those true friends who had stayed with him in his banishment; and these worthy followers, though they had patiently shared his adverse fortune, were very well pleased to return in peace and prosperity to the palace of their lawful duke.

THE MERCHANT OF VENICE

Shylock, the Jew, lived at Venice: he was an usurer, who had amassed an immense fortune by lending money at great interest to Christian merchants. Shylock, being a hard-hearted man, exacted the payment of the money he lent with such severity that he was much disliked by all good men, and particularly by Antonio, a young merchant of Venice; and Shylock as much hated Antonio, because he used to lend money to people in distress, and would never take any interest for the money he lent; therefore there was great enmity between this covetous Jew and the generous merchant Antonio. Whenever Antonio met Shylock on the Rialto (or Exchange), he used to reproach him with his usuries and hard dealings, which the Jew would bear with seeming patience, while he secretly meditated revenge.

Antonio was the kindest man that lived, the best conditioned, and had the most unwearied spirit in doing courtesies; indeed, he was one in whom the ancient Roman honour more appeared than in any that drew breath in Italy. He was greatly beloved by all his fellow-citizens; but the friend who was nearest and dearest to his heart was Bassanio, a noble Venetian, who, having but a small patrimony, had nearly exhausted his little fortune by living in too expensive a manner for his slender means, as young men of high rank with small fortunes are too apt to do. Whenever Bassanio wanted money, Antonio assisted him;

and it seemed as if they had but one heart and one purse between them.

One day Bassanio came to Antonio, and told him that he wished to repair his fortune by a wealthy marriage with a lady whom he dearly loved, whose father, that was lately dead, had left her sole heiress to a large estate; and that in her father's lifetime he used to visit at her house, when he thought he had observed this lady had some-times from her eyes sent speechless messages, that seemed to say he would be no unwelcome suitor; but not having money to furnish himself with an appearance befit-ting the lover of so rich an heiress, he besought Antonio to add to the many favours he had shown him, by lending him three thousand ducats.

Antonio had no money by him at that time to lend his friend; but expecting soon to have some ships come home laden with merchandise, he said he would go to Shylock, the rich money-lender and borrow the money upon the credit of those ships.

Antonio and Bassanio went together to Shylock, and Antonio asked the Jew to lend him three thousand ducats upon any interest he should require, to be paid out of the merchandise contained in his ships at sea. On this, Shylock thought within himself: 'If I can once catch him on the hip, I will feed fat the ancient grudge I bear him; he hates our Jewish nation; he lends out money gratis, and among mer-chants he rails at me and my well-earned bargains, which he calls interest. Cursed be my tribe if I forgive him!' Anto-nio finding he was musing within himself and did not answer, and being impatient for the money, said: 'Shylock, do you hear? will you lend the money?' To this question the Jew replied: 'Signior Antonio, on the Rialto many a time and often you have railed at me about my monies and my usuries, and I have borne it with a patient shrug, for suffer-ance is the badge of all our tribe; and then you have called me unbeliever, cut-throat dog, and spit upon my Jewish garments, and spurned at me with your foot, as if I was a cur. Well then, it now appears you need my help; and you come to me, and say, *Shylock, lend me monies*. Has a dog money? Is it possible a cur should lend three thousand ducats? Shall I bend low and say, Fair sir, you spit upon me on Wednesday last, another time you called me dog, and for these courtesies I am to lend you monies.' Antonio replied: 'I am as like to call you so again, to spit on you again, and spurn you too. If you will lend me this money, lend it not to me as to a friend, but rather lend it to me as to an enemy, that, if I break, you may with better face exact the penalty.' 'Why, look you,' said Shylock, 'how you storm! I would be friends with you, and have your love. I will forget the shames you have put upon me. I will supply your wants, and take no interest for my money.' This seemingly kind offer greatly surprised Antonio; and then Shylock, still pretending kindness, and that all he did was to gain Antonio's love, again said he would lend him the three thousand ducats, and take no interest for his money; only Antonio should go with him to a lawyer, and there sign in merry sport a bond, that if he did not repay the money by a certain day, he would forfeit a pound of flesh, to be cut off from any part of his body that Shylock pleased.

'Content,' said Antonio: 'I will sign to this bond, and say there is much kindness in the Jew.'

Bassanio said Antonio should not sign to such a bond for him; but still Antonio insisted that he would sign it, for that before the day of payment came, his ships would return laden with many times the value of the money.

Shylock, hearing this debate, exclaimed: 'O, father Abraham, what suspicious people these Christians are! Their own hard dealings teach them to suspect the thoughts of others. I pray you tell me this, Bassanio: if he should break this day, what should I gain by the exaction of the forfeiture? A pound of man's flesh, taken from a man, is not so estimable, nor profitable neither, as the flesh of mutton or beef. I say, to buy his favour I offer this friendship: if he will take it, so; if not, adieu.'

At last, against the advice of Bassanio, who, notwithstanding all the Jew had said of his kind intentions, did not like his friend should run the hazard of this shocking penalty for his sake, Antonio signed the bond, thinking it really was (as the Jew said) merely in sport.

The rich heiress that Bassanio wished to marry lived near Venice, at a place called Belmont: her name was Portia, and in the graces of her person and her mind she was nothing inferior to that Portia, of whom we read, who was Cato's daughter, and the wife of Brutus.

Bassanio being so kindly supplied with money by his friend Antonio, at the hazard of his life, set out for Belmont with a splendid train, and attended by a gentleman of the name of Gratiano.

Bassanio proving successful in his suit, Portia in a short time consented to accept of him for a husband.

Bassanio confessed to Portia that he had no fortune, and that his high birth and noble ancestry was all that he could boast of; she, who loved him for his worthy qualities, and had riches enough not to regard wealth in a husband, answered with a graceful modesty, that she would wish herself a thousand times more fair, and ten thousand times more rich, to be more worthy of him; and then the accomplished Portia prettily dispraised herself, and said she was an unlessoned girl, unschooled, unpractised, yet not so old but that she could learn, and that she would commit her gentle spirit to be directed and governed by him in all things; and she said: 'Myself and what is mine, to you and yours is now converted. But yesterday, Bassanio, I was the lady of this fair mansion, queen of myself, and mistress over these servants; and now this house, these servants, and myself, are yours, my lord; I give them with this ring'; presenting a ring to Bassanio.

Bassanio was so overpowered with gratitude and wonder at the gracious manner in which the rich and noble Portia accepted of a man of his humble fortunes, that he could not express his joy and reverence to the dear lady who so honoured him, by anything but broken words of love and thankfulness; and taking the ring, he vowed never to part with it.

Gratiano and Nerissa, Portia's waiting-maid, were in attendance upon their lord and lady, when Portia so gracefully promised to become the obedient wife of Bassanio; and Gratiano, wishing Bassanio and the generous lady joy, desired permission to be married at the same time.

'With all my heart, Gratiano,' said Bassanio, 'if you can get a wife.'

Gratiano then said that he loved the lady Portia's fair waiting gentlewoman Nerissa, and that she had promised to be his wife, if her lady married Bassanio. Portia asked Nerissa if this was true. Nerissa replied: 'Madam, it is so, if you approve of it.' Portia willingly consenting, Bassanio pleasantly said: 'Then our wedding-feast shall be much honoured by your marriage, Gratiano.'

The happiness of these lovers was sadly crossed at this moment by the entrance of a messenger, who brought a letter from Antonio containing fearful tidings. When Bassanio read Antonio's letter, Portia feared it was to tell him of the death of some dear friend, he looked so pale; and inquiring what was the news which had so distressed him, he said: 'O sweet Portia, here are a few of the unpleasantest words that ever blotted paper; gentle lady, when I first imparted my love to you, I freely told you all the wealth I had ran in my veins; but I should have told you that I had less than nothing, being in debt.' Bassanio then told Portia what has been here related, of his borrowing the money of Antonio, and of Antonio's procuring it of Shylock the Jew, and of the bond by which Antonio had engaged to forfeit a pound of flesh, if it was not repaid by a certain day: and then Bassanio read Antonio's letter: the words of which were: *Sweet Bassanio, my ships are all lost, my bond to the Jew is forfeited, and since in paying it is impossible I should live, I could wish to see you at my death; notwithstanding use your pleasure; if your love for me do not persuade you to come, let not my letter.'* 'O, my dear love,' said Portia, 'despatch all business, and begone; you shall have gold to pay the money twenty times over, before this kind friend shall lose a hair by my Bassanio's fault; and as you are so dearly bought, I will dearly love you.' Portia then said she would be married to Bassanio before he set out, to give him a legal right to her money; and that same day they were married, and Gratiano was also married to Nerissa; and Bassanio and Gratiano, the instant they were married, set out in great haste for Venice, where Bassanio found Antonio in prison.

The day of payment being past, the cruel Jew would not accept of the money which Bassanio offered him, but insisted upon having a pound of Antonio's flesh. A day was appointed to try this shocking cause before the duke of Venice, and Bassanio awaited in dreadful suspense the event of the trial.

When Portia parted with her husband, she spoke cheeringly to him, and bade him bring his dear friend along with him when he returned; yet she feared it would go hard with Antonio, and when she was left alone, she began to think and consider within herself, if she could by any means be instrumental in saving the life of her dear Bassanio's friend; and notwithstanding when she wished to honour her Bassanio, she had said to him with such a meek and wifelike grace, that she would submit in all things to be governed by his superior wisdom, yet being now called forth into action by the peril of her honoured husband's friend, she did nothing doubt her own powers, and by the sole guidance of her own true and perfect judgement, at once resolved to go herself to Venice, and speak in Antonio's defence.

Portia had a relation who was a counsellor in the law; to this gentleman, whose name was Bellario, she wrote, and stating the case to him, desired his opinion, and that with his advice he would also send her the dress worn by a counsellor. When the messenger returned, he brought letters from Bellario of advice how to proceed, and also everything necessary for her equipment.

Portia dressed herself and her maid Nerissa in men's apparel, and putting on the robes of a counsellor, she took

Nerissa along with her as her clerk; and setting out immediately, they arrived at Venice on the very day of the trial.
The cause was just going to be heard before the duke and
senators of Venice in the senate-house, when Portia
entered this high court of justice, and presented a letter
from Bellario, in which that learned counsellor wrote to
the duke, saying, he would have come himself to plead for
Antonio, but that he was prevented by sickness, and he
requested that the learned young doctor Balthasar (so he
called Portia) might be permitted to plead in his stead.
This the duke granted, much wondering at the youthful
appearance of the stranger, who was prettily disguised by
her counsellor's robes and her large wig.

And now began this important trial. Portia looked
around her, and she knew the merciless Jew; and she saw
Bassanio, but he knew her not in her disguise. He was
standing beside Antonio, in an agony of distress and fear
for his friend.

The importance of the arduous task Portia had engaged
in gave this tender lady courage, and she boldly proceeded in the duty she had undertaken to perform: and
first of all she addressed herself to Shylock; and allowing
that he had a right by the Venetian law to have the forfeit
expressed in the bond, she spoke so sweetly of the noble
quality of *mercy,* as would have softened any heart but the
unfeeling Shylock's; saying, that it dropped as the gentle
rain from heaven upon the place beneath; and how mercy
was a double blessing, it blessed him that gave, and him
that received it; and how it became monarchs better than
their crowns, being an attribute of God Himself; and that
earthly power came nearest to God's, in proportion as
mercy tempered justice; and she bid Shylock remember
that as we all pray for mercy, that same prayer should
teach us to show mercy. Shylock only answered her by
desiring to have the penalty forfeited in the bond. 'Is he
not able to pay the money?' asked Portia. Bassanio then
offered the Jew the payment of the three thousand ducats
as many times over as he should desire; which Shylock

refusing, and still insisting upon having a pound of Antonio's flesh, Bassanio begged the learned young counsellor would endeavour to wrest the law a little, to save Antonio's life. But Portia gravely answered, that laws once established must never be altered. Shylock hearing Portia say that the law might not be altered, it seemed to him that she was pleading in his favour, and he said: 'A Daniel is come to judgement! O wise young judge, how I do honour you! How much elder are you than your looks!'

Portia now desired Shylock to let her look at the bond; and when she had read it, she said: 'This bond is forfeited, and by this the Jew may lawfully claim a pound of flesh, to be by him cut off nearest Antonio's heart.' Then she said to Shylock: 'Be merciful: take the money, and bid me tear the bond.' But no mercy would the cruel Shylock show; and he said: 'By my soul I swear, there is no power in the tongue of men to alter me.' 'Why then, Antonio,' said Portia, 'you must prepare your bosom for the knife': and while Shylock was sharpening a long knife with great eagerness to cut off the pound of flesh, Portia said to Antonio: 'Have you anything to say?' Antonio with a calm resignation replied, that he had but little to say, for that he had prepared his mind for death. Then he said to Bassanio: 'Give me your hand, Bassanio! Fare you well! Grieve not that I am fallen into this misfortune for you. Commend me to your honourable wife, and tell her how I have loved you!' Bassanio in the deepest affliction replied: 'Antonio, I am married to a wife, who is as dear to me as life itself; but life itself, my wife, and all the world, are not esteemed with me above your life; I would lose all, I would sacrifice all to this devil here, to deliver you.'

Portia hearing this, though the kind-hearted lady was not at all offended with her husband for expressing the love he owed to so true a friend as Antonio in these strong terms, yet could not help answering: 'Your wife would give you little thanks, if she were present, to hear you make this offer.' And then Gratiano, who loved to copy what his lord did, thought he must make a speech like

Bassanio's, and he said, in Nerissa's hearing, who was writing in her clerk's dress by the side of Portia: 'I have a wife, whom I protest I love; I wish she were in heaven, if she could but entreat some power there to change the cruel temper of this currish Jew.' 'It is well you wish this behind her back, else you would have but an unquiet house,' said Nerissa.

Shylock now cried out impatiently: 'We trifle time; I pray pronounce the sentence.' And now all was awful expectation in the court, and every heart was full of grief for Antonio.

Portia asked if the scales were ready to weigh the flesh; and she said to the Jew: 'Shylock, you must have some surgeon by, lest he bleed to death.' Shylock, whose whole intent was that Antonio should bleed to death, said: 'It is not so named in the bond.' Portia replied: 'It is not so named in the bond, but what of that? It were good you did so much for charity.' To this all the answer Shylock would make was: 'I cannot find it; it is not in the bond.' 'Then,' said Portia, 'a pound of Antonio's flesh is thine. The law allows it, and the court awards it. And you may cut this flesh from off his breast. The law allows it and the court awards it.' Again Shylock exclaimed: 'O wise and upright judge! A Daniel is come to judgement!' And then he sharpened his long knife again, and looking eagerly on Antonio, he said: 'Come, prepare!'

'Tarry a little, Jew,' said Portia; 'there is something else. This bond here gives you no drop of blood; the words expressly are "a pound of flesh." If in the cutting off the pound of flesh you shed one drop of Christian blood, your lands and goods are by the law to be confiscated to the state of Venice.' Now as it was utterly impossible for Shylock to cut off the pound of flesh without shedding some of Antonio's blood, this wise discovery of Portia's, that it was flesh and not blood that was named in the bond, saved the life of Antonio; and all admiring the wonderful sagacity of the young counsellor, who had so happily thought of this expedient, plaudits resounded from every part of the senate-house; and Gratiano exclaimed, in the words which Shylock had used: 'O wise and upright judge! mark, Jew, a Daniel is come to judgement!'

Shylock, finding himself defeated in his cruel intent, said with a disappointed look, that he would take the money; and Bassanio, rejoiced beyond measure at Antonio's unexpected deliverance, cried out: 'Here is the money!' But Portia stopped him, saying: 'Softly; there is no haste; the Jew shall have nothing but the penalty: therefore prepare, Shylock, to cut off the flesh; but mind you shed no blood: nor do not cut off more nor less than just a pound; be it more or less by one poor scruple, nay if the scale turn but by the weight of a single hair, you are condemned by the laws of Venice to die, and all your wealth is forfeited to the senate.' 'Give me my money, and let me go,' said Shylock. 'I have it ready,' said Bassanio: 'here it is.'

Shylock was going to take the money, when Portia again stopped him, saying: 'Tarry, Jew; I have yet another hold upon you. By the laws of Venice, your wealth is forfeited to the state, for having conspired against the life of one of its citizens, and your life lies at the mercy of the duke; therefore, down on your knees, and ask him to pardon you.'

The duke then said to Shylock: 'That you may see the difference of our Christian spirit, I pardon you your life before you ask it; half your wealth belongs to Antonio, the other half comes to the state.'

The generous Antonio then said that he would give up his share of Shylock's wealth, if Shylock would sign a deed to make it over at his death to his daughter and her husband; for Antonio knew that the Jew had an only daughter who had lately married against his consent to a young Christian, named Lorenzo, a friend of Antonio's, which had so offended Shylock, that he had disinherited her.

The Jew agreed to this: and being thus disappointed in his revenge, and despoiled of his riches, he said: 'I am ill. Let me go home; send the deed after me, and I will sign over half my riches to my daughter.' 'Get thee gone, then,' said the duke, 'and sign it; and if you repent your cruelty and turn Christian, the state will forgive you the fine of the other half of your riches.'

The duke now released Antonio, and dismissed the court. He then highly praised the wisdom and ingenuity of the young counsellor, and invited him home to dinner. Portia, who meant to return to Belmont before her husband, replied: 'I humbly thank your grace, but I must away directly.' The duke said he was sorry he had not leisure to stay and dine with him; and turning to Antonio, he added: 'Reward this gentleman; for in my mind you are much indebted to him.'

The duke and his senators left the court; and then Bassanio said to Portia: 'Most worthy gentleman, I and my friend Antonio have by your wisdom been this day acquitted of grievous penalties, and I beg you will accept of the three thousand ducats due unto the Jew.' 'And we shall stand indebted to you over and above,' said Antonio, 'in love and service evermore.'

Portia could not be prevailed upon to accept the money; but upon Bassanio still pressing her to accept of some reward, she said: 'Give me your gloves; I will wear them for your sake'; and then Bassanio taking off his gloves, she espied the ring which she had given him upon his finger: now it was the ring the wily lady wanted to get from him to make a merry jest when she saw her Bassanio again, that made her ask him for his gloves; and she said, when she saw the ring, 'and for your love I will take this ring from you.' Bassanio was sadly distressed that the counsellor should ask him for the only thing he could not part with, and he replied in great confusion, that he could not give him that ring, because it was his wife's gift, and he had vowed never to part with it; but that he would give him the most valuable ring in Venice, and find it out by proclamation. On this Portia affected to be affronted, and left the court, saying: 'You teach me, sir, how a beggar should be answered.'

'Dear Bassanio,' said Antonio, 'let him have the ring; let my love and the great service he has done for me be valued against your wife's displeasure.' Bassanio, ashamed to appear so ungrateful, yielded, and sent Gratiano after Portia with the ring; and then the *clerk* Nerissa, who had also given Gratiano a ring, she begged his ring, and Gratiano (not choosing to be outdone in generosity by his lord) gave it to her. And there was laughing among these ladies to think, when they got home, how they would tax their husbands with giving away their rings, and swear that they had given them as a present to some woman.

Portia, when she returned, was in that happy temper of mind which never fails to attend the consciousness of having performed a good action; her cheerful spirits enjoyed everything she saw: the moon never seemed to shine so bright before; and when that pleasant moon was hid behind a cloud, then a light which she saw from her house at Belmont as well pleased her charmed fancy, and she said to Nerissa: 'That light we see is burning in my hall; how far that little candle throws its beams, so shines a good deed in a naughty world'; and hearing the sound of music from her house, she said: 'Methinks that music sounds much sweeter than by day.'

And now Portia and Nerissa entered the house, and dressing themselves in their own apparel, they awaited the arrival of their husbands, who soon followed them with Antonio; and Bassanio presenting his dear friend to the lady Portia, the congratulations and welcomings of that lady were hardly over, when they perceived Nerissa and her husband quarrelling in a corner of the room. 'A quarrel already?' said Portia. 'What is the matter?' Gratiano replied: 'Lady, it is about a paltry gilt ring that Nerissa gave me, with words upon it like the poetry on a cutler's knife; *Love me, and leave me not.*'

'What does the poetry or the value of the ring signify?' said Nerissa. 'You swore to me when I gave it to you, that you would keep it till the hour of death; and now you say you gave it to the lawyer's clerk. I know you gave it to a woman.' 'By this hand,' replied Gratiano, 'I gave it to a youth, a kind of boy, a little scrubbed boy, no higher than yourself; he was clerk to the young counsellor that by his wise pleading saved Antonio's life: this prating boy begged it for a fee, and I could not for my life deny him.' Portia said: 'You were to blame, Gratiano, to part with your wife's first gift. I gave my lord Bassanio a ring, and I am sure he would not part with it for all the world.' Gratiano, in excuse for his fault, now said: 'My lord Bassanio gave his ring away to the counsellor, and then the boy, his clerk, that took some pains in writing, he begged my ring.'

Portia, hearing this, seemed very angry, and reproached Bassanio for giving away her ring; and she said, Nerissa had taught her what to believe, and that she knew some woman had the ring. Bassanio was very unhappy to have so offended his dear lady, and he said with great earnestness: 'No, by my honour, no woman had it, but a civil doctor, who refused three thousand ducats of me, and begged the ring, which when I denied him, he went displeased away. What could I do, sweet Portia? I was so beset with shame for my seeming ingratitude, that I was forced to send the ring after him. Pardon me, good lady; had you been there, I think you would have begged the ring of me to give the worthy doctor.'

'Ah!' said Antonio, 'I am the unhappy cause of these quarrels.'

Portia bid Antonio not to grieve at that, for that he was welcome notwithstanding; and then Antonio said: 'I once did lend my body for Bassanio's sake; and but for him to whom your husband gave the ring, I should have now been dead. I dare be bound again, my soul upon the forfeit, your lord will never more break his faith with you.' 'Then you shall be his surety,' said Portia; 'give him this ring, and bid him keep it better than the other.'

When Bassanio looked at this ring, he was strangely surprised to find it was the same he gave away; and then

Portia told him how she was the young counsellor, and Nerissa was her clerk; and Bassanio found, to his unspeakable wonder and delight, that it was by the noble courage and wisdom of his wife that Antonio's life was saved.

And Portia again welcomed Antonio, and gave him letters which by some chance had fallen into her hands, which contained an account of Antonio's ships, that were supposed lost, being safely arrived in the harbour. So these tragical beginnings of this rich merchant's story were all forgotten in the unexpected good fortune which ensued; and there was leisure to laugh at the comical adventure of the rings, and the husbands that did not know their own wives: Gratiano merrily swearing, in a sort of rhyming speech, that

> . . . while he lived, he'd fear no other thing
> So sore, as keeping safe Nerissa's ring.

KING LEAR

Lear, king of Britain, had three daughters; Goneril, wife
to the duke of Albany; Regan, wife to the duke of
Cornwall; and Cordelia, a young maid, for whose love the
king of France and duke of Burgundy were joint suitors,
and were at this time making stay for that purpose in the
court of Lear.

The old king, worn out with age and the fatigues of government, he being more than fourscore years old, determined to take no further part in state affairs, but to leave
the management to younger strengths, that he might have
time to prepare for death, which must at no long period
ensue. With this intent he called his three daughters to
him, to know from their own lips which of them loved him
best, that he might part his kingdom among them in such
proportions as their affection for him should seem to
deserve.

Goneril, the eldest, declared that she loved her father
more than words could give out, that he was dearer to her
than the light of her own eyes, dearer than life and liberty,
with a deal of such professing stuff, which is easy to counterfeit where there is no real love, only a few fine words
delivered with confidence being wanted in that case. The
king, delighted to hear from her own mouth this assurance of her love, and thinking truly that her heart went
with it, in a fit of fatherly fondness bestowed upon her and
her husband one-third of his ample kingdom.

Then calling to him his second daughter, he demanded

what she had to say. Regan, who was made of the same
hollow metal as her sister, was not a whit behind in her
profession, but rather declared that what her sister had
spoken came short of the love which she professed to
bear for his highness; insomuch that she found all other
joys dead, in comparison with the pleasure which she
took in the love of her dear king and father.

Lear blessed himself in having such loving children, as
he thought; and could do no less, after the handsome
assurances which Regan had made, than bestow a third of
his kingdom upon her and her husband, equal in size to
that which he had already given away to Goneril.

Then turning to his youngest daughter Cordelia, whom
he called his joy, he asked what she had to say, thinking
no doubt that she would glad his ears with the same loving speeches which her sisters had uttered, or rather that
her expressions would be so much stronger than theirs,
as she had always been his darling, and favoured by him
above either of them. But Cordelia, disgusted with the
flattery of her sisters, whose hearts she knew were far
from their lips, and seeing that all their coaxing speeches
were only intended to wheedle the old king out of his
dominions, that they and their husbands might reign in
his lifetime, made no other reply but this—that she loved
his majesty according to her duty, neither more nor less.

The king, shocked with this appearance of ingratitude
in his favourite child, desired her to consider her words,
and to mend her speech, lest it should mar her fortunes.

Cordelia then told her father, that he was her father,
that he had given her breeding, and loved her; that she
returned those duties back as was most fit, and did obey
him, love him, and most honour him. But that she could
not frame her mouth to such large speeches as her sisters
had done, or promise to love nothing else in the world.
Why had her sisters husbands, if (as they said) they had
no love for anything but their father? If she should ever
wed, she was sure the lord to whom she gave her hand

would want half her love, half of her care and duty; she should never marry like her sisters, to love her father all.

Cordelia, who in earnest loved her old father even almost as extravagantly as her sisters pretended to do, would have plainly told him so at any other time, in more daughter-like and loving terms, and without these qualifications, which did indeed sound a little ungracious; but after the crafty flattering speeches of her sisters, which she had seen draw such extravagant rewards, she thought the handsomest thing she could do was to love and be silent. This put her affection out of suspicion of mercenary ends, and showed that she loved, but not for gain; and that her professions, the less ostentatious they were, had so much the more of truth and sincerity than her sisters'.

This plainness of speech, which Lear called pride, so enraged the old monarch—who in his best of times always showed much of spleen and rashness, and in whom the dotage incident to old age had so clouded over his reason, that he could not discern truth from flattery, nor a gay painted speech from words that came from the heart—that in a fury of resentment he retracted the third part of his kingdom, which yet remained, and which he had reserved for Cordelia, and gave it away from her, sharing it equally between her two sisters and their husbands, the dukes of Albany and Cornwall; whom he now called to him, and in presence of all his courtiers bestowing a coronet between them, invested them jointly with all the power, revenue, and execution of government, only retaining to himself the name of king; all the rest of royalty he resigned; with this reservation, that himself, with a hundred knights for his attendants, was to be maintained by monthly course in each of his daughters' palaces in turn.

So preposterous a disposal of his kingdom, so little guided by reason, and so much by passion, filled all his courtiers with astonishment and sorrow; but none of them had the courage to interpose between this incensed king and his wrath, except the earl of Kent, who was beginning to speak a good word for Cordelia, when the passionate Lear on pain of death commanded him to desist; but the good Kent was not so to be repelled. He had been ever loyal to Lear, whom he had honoured as a king, loved as a father, followed as a master; and he had never esteemed his life further than as a pawn to wage against his royal master's enemies, nor feared to lose it when Lear's safety was the motive; nor now that Lear was most his own enemy, did this faithful servant of the king forget his old principles, but manfully opposed Lear, to do Lear good; and was unmannerly only because Lear was mad. He had been a most faithful counsellor in times past to the king, and he besought him now, that he would see with his eyes (as he had done in many weighty matters), and go by his advice still; and in his best consideration recall this hideous rashness: for he would answer with his life, his judgement that Lear's youngest daughter did not love him least, nor were those empty-hearted whose low sound gave no token of hollowness. When power bowed to flattery, honour was bound to plainness. For Lear's threats, what could he do to him, whose life was already at his service? That should not hinder duty from speaking.

The honest freedom of this good earl of Kent only stirred up the king's wrath the more, and like a frantic patient who kills his physician, and loves his mortal disease, he banished this true servant, and allotted him but five days to make his preparations for departure; but if on the sixth his hated person was found within the realm of Britain, that moment was to be his death. And Kent bade farewell to the king, and said, that since he chose to show himself in such fashion, it was but banishment to stay there; and before he went, he recommended Cordelia to the protection of the gods, the maid who had so rightly thought, and so discreetly spoken; and only wished that her sisters' large speeches might be answered with deeds of love; and then he went, as he said, to shape his old course to a new country.

The king of France and duke of Burgundy were now called in to hear the determination of Lear about his youngest daughter, and to know whether they would persist in their courtship to Cordelia, now that she was under her father's displeasure, and had no fortune but her own person to recommend her: and the duke of Burgundy declined the match, and would not take her to wife upon such conditions; but the king of France, understanding what the nature of the fault had been which had lost her the love of her father, that it was only a tardiness of speech, and the not being able to frame her tongue to flattery like her sisters, took this young maid by the hand, and saying that her virtues were a dowry above a kingdom, bade Cordelia to take farewell of her sisters and of her father, though he had been unkind, and she should go with him, and be queen of him and of fair France, and reign over fairer possessions than her sisters: and he called the duke of Burgundy in contempt a waterish duke, because his love for this young maid had in a moment run all away like water.

Then Cordelia with weeping eyes took leave of her sisters, and besought them to love their father well, and make good their professions: and they sullenly told her not to prescribe to them, for they knew their duty; but to strive to content her husband, who had taken her (as they tauntingly expressed it) as Fortune's alms. And Cordelia with a heavy heart departed, for she knew the cunning of her sisters, and she wished her father in better hands than she was about to leave him in.

Cordelia was no sooner gone, than the devilish dispositions of her sisters began to show themselves in their true colours. Even before the expiration of the first month, which Lear was to spend by agreement with his eldest daughter Goneril, the old king began to find out the difference between promises and performances. This wretch having got from her father all that he had to bestow, even to the giving away of the crown from off his head, began to grudge even those small remnants of royalty which the old man had reserved to himself, to please his fancy with the idea of being still a king. She could not bear to see him and his hundred knights. Every time she met her father, she put on a frowning countenance; and when the old man wanted to speak with her, she would feign sickness, or anything to get rid of the sight of him; for it was plain that she esteemed his old age a useless burden, and his attendants an unnecessary expense: not only she herself slackened in her expressions of duty to the king, but by her example, and (it is to be feared) not without her private instructions, her very servants affected to treat him with neglect, and would either refuse to obey his orders, or still more contemptuously pretend not to hear them. Lear could not but perceive this alteration in the behaviour of his daughter, but he shut his eyes against it as long as he could, as people commonly are unwilling to believe the unpleasant consequences which their own mistakes and obstinacy have brought upon them.

True love and fidelity are no more to be estranged by *ill,* than falsehood and hollow-heartedness can be conciliated by *good, usage.* This eminently appears in the instance of the good earl of Kent, who, though banished by Lear, and his life made forfeit if he were found in Britain, chose to stay and abide all consequences, as long as there was a chance of his being useful to the king his master. See to what mean shifts and disguises poor loyalty is forced to submit sometimes; yet it counts nothing base or unworthy, so as it can but do service where it owes an obligation! In the disguise of a serving man, all his greatness and pomp laid aside, this good earl proffered his services to the king, who, not knowing him to be Kent in that disguise, but pleased with a certain plainness, or rather bluntness in his answers, which the earl put on (so different from that smooth oily flattery which he had so much reason to be sick of, having found the effects not answerable in his daughter), a bargain was quickly struck, and Lear took Kent into his service by the name of Caius, as he called himself, never suspecting him to be his once great favourite, the high and mighty earl of Kent.

This Caius quickly found means to show his fidelity and love to his royal master: for Goneril's steward that same day behaving in a disrespectful manner to Lear, and giving him saucy looks and language, as no doubt he was secretly encouraged to do by his mistress, Caius, not enduring to hear so open an affront put upon his majesty, made no more ado but presently tripped up his heels, and laid the unmannerly slave in the kennel; for which friendly service Lear became more and more attached to him.

Nor was Kent the only friend Lear had. In his degree, and as far as so insignificant a personage could show his love, the poor fool, or jester, that had been of his palace while Lear had a palace, as it was the custom of kings and great personages at that time to keep a fool (as he was called) to make them sport after serious business: this poor fool clung to Lear after he had given away his crown, and by his witty sayings would keep up his good humour, though he could not refrain sometimes from jeering at his master for his imprudence in uncrowning himself, and giving all away to his daughters; at which time, as he rhymingly expressed it, these daughters

> For sudden joy did weep
>   And he for sorrow sung,
> That such a king should play bo-peep
>   And go the fools among.

And in such wild sayings, and scraps of songs, of which he had plenty, this pleasant honest fool poured out his heart even in the presence of Goneril herself, in many a bitter taunt and jest which cut to the quick: such as comparing the king to the hedge-sparrow, who feeds the young of the cuckoo till they grow old enough, and then has its head bit off for its pains; and saying, that an ass may know when the cart draws the horse (meaning that Lear's daughters, that ought to go behind, now ranked before their father); and that Lear was no longer Lear, but the shadow of Lear: for which free speeches he was once or twice threatened to be whipped.

The coolness and falling off of respect which Lear had begun to perceive, were not all which this foolish fond father was to suffer from his unworthy daughter: she now plainly told him that his staying in her palace was inconvenient so long as he insisted upon keeping up an establishment of a hundred knights; that this establishment was useless and expensive, and only served to fill her court with riot and feasting; and she prayed him that he would lessen their number, and keep none but old men about him, such as himself, and fitting his age.

Lear at first could not believe his eyes or ears, nor that it was his daughter who spoke so unkindly. He could not believe that she who had received a crown from him could seek to cut off his train, and grudge him the respect due to his old age. But she persisting in her undutiful demand, the old man's rage was so excited, that he called her a detested kite, and said that she spoke an untruth; and so indeed she did, for the hundred knights were all men of choice behaviour and sobriety of manners, skilled in all particulars of duty, and not given to rioting or feasting, as she said. And he bid his horses to be prepared, for he would go to his other daughter, Regan, he and his hundred knights; and he spoke of ingratitude, and said it was a marble-hearted devil, and showed more hideous in a child than the sea-monster. And he cursed his eldest daughter Goneril so as was terrible to hear; praying that she might never have a child, or if she had, that it might live to return that scorn and contempt upon her which she had shown to him: that she might feel how sharper than a serpent's tooth it was to have a thankless child. And Goneril's husband, the duke of Albany, beginning to excuse himself for any share which Lear might suppose he had in the unkindness, Lear would not hear him out, but in a rage ordered his horses to be saddled, and set out with his followers for the abode of Regan, his other daughter. And Lear thought to himself how small the fault of Cordelia (if it was a fault) now appeared, in comparison with her sister's, and he wept; and then he was ashamed that such a creature as Goneril should have so much power over his manhood as to make him weep.

Regan and her husband were keeping their court in great pomp and state at their palace; and Lear despatched his servant Caius with letters to his daughter, that she might be prepared for his reception, while he and his train followed after. But it seems that Goneril had been beforehand with him, sending letters also to Regan, accusing her father of waywardness and ill humours, and advising her not to receive so great a train as he was bringing with him. This messenger arrived at the same time with Caius, and Caius and he met: and who should it be but Caius's old enemy the steward, whom he had formerly tripped up by the heels for his saucy behaviour to Lear. Caius not liking the fellow's look, and suspecting what he came for, began to revile him, and challenged him to fight, which the fellow refusing, Caius, in a fit of honest passion, beat him soundly, as such a mischief-maker and carrier of wicked messages deserved; which coming to the ears of Regan and her husband, they ordered Caius to be put in the stocks, though he was a messenger from the king her father, and in that character demanded the highest respect: so that the first thing the king saw when he entered the castle, was his faithful servant Caius sitting in that disgraceful situation.

This was but a bad omen of the reception which he was to expect; but a worse followed, when, upon inquiry for his daughter and her husband, he was told they were weary with travelling all night, and could not see him; and when lastly, upon his insisting in a positive and angry manner to see them, they came to greet him, whom should he see in their company but the hated Goneril, who had come to tell her own story, and set her sister against the king her father!

This sight much moved the old man, and still more to see Regan take her by the hand; and he asked Goneril if she was not ashamed to look upon his old white beard. And Regan advised him to go home again with Goneril, and live with her peaceably, dismissing half of his attendants, and to ask her forgiveness; for he was old and wanted discretion, and must be ruled and led by persons that had more discretion than himself. And Lear showed how preposterous that would sound, if he were to go down on his knees, and beg of his own daughter for food and raiment, and he argued against such an unnatural dependence, declaring his resolution never to return with her, but to stay where he was with Regan, he and his hundred knights; for he said that she had not forgot the half of the kingdom which he had endowed her with, and that her eyes were not fierce like Goneril's, but mild and kind. And he said that rather than return to Goneril, with half his train cut off, he would go over to France, and beg a wretched pension of the king there, who had married his youngest daughter without a portion.

But he was mistaken in expecting kinder treatment of Regan than he had experienced from her sister Goneril. As if willing to outdo her sister in unfilial behaviour, she declared that she thought fifty knights too many to wait upon him: that five-and-twenty were enough. Then Lear, nigh heart-broken, turned to Goneril and said that he would go back with her, for her fifty doubled five-and-twenty, and so her love was twice as much as Regan's. But Goneril excused herself, and said, what need of so many as five-and-twenty? or even ten? or five? when he might be waited upon by her servants, or her sister's servants? So these two wicked daughters, as if they strove to exceed each other in cruelty to their old father, who had been so good to them, by little and little would have abated him of all his train, all respect (little enough for him that once commanded a kingdom), which was left him to show that he had once been a king! Not that a splendid train is essential to happiness, but from a king to a beggar is a hard change, from commanding millions to be without one attendant; and it was the ingratitude in his daughters' denying it, more than what he would suffer by the want of it, which pierced this poor king to the heart; insomuch, that with this double ill-usage, a vexation for having so foolishly given away a kingdom, his wits began to be unsettled, and while he said he knew not what, he vowed revenge against those unnatural hags, and to make examples of them that should be a terror to the earth!

While he was thus idly threatening what his weak arm could never execute, night came on, and a loud storm of thunder and lightning with rain; and his daughters still persisting in their resolution not to admit his followers, he called for his horses, and chose rather to encounter the utmost fury of the storm abroad, than stay under the same roof with these ungrateful daughters: and they, saying that the injuries which wilful men procure to themselves are their just punishment, suffered him to go in that condition and shut their doors upon him.

The wind were high, and the rain and storm increased, when the old man sallied forth to combat with the elements, less sharp than his daughters' unkindness. For many miles about there was scarce a bush; and there upon a heath, exposed to the fury of the storm in a dark night, did king Lear wander out, and defy the winds and the thunder; and he bid the winds to blow the earth into the sea, or swell the waves of the sea till they drowned the earth, that no token might remain of any such ungrateful animal as man. The old king was now left with no other companion than the poor fool, who still abided with him, with his merry conceits striving to outjest misfortune, saying it was but a naughty night to swim in, and truly the king had better go in and ask his daughters' blessing:

> But he that has a little tiny wit,
>   With heigh ho, the wind and the rain!
> Must make content with his fortunes fit,
>   Though the rain it raineth every day:

and swearing it was a brave night to cool a lady's pride.

Thus poorly accompanied, this once great monarch was found by his ever-faithful servant the good earl of Kent, now transformed to Caius, who ever followed close at his side, though the king did not know him to be the earl; and he said: 'Alas! sir, are you here? creatures that love night, love not such nights as these. This dreadful storm has driven the beasts to their hiding places. Man's nature cannot endure the affliction or the fear.' And Lear rebuked him and said, these lesser evils were not felt, where a greater malady was fixed. When the mind is at ease, the body has leisure to be delicate, but the temper in his mind did take all feeling else from his senses, but of that which beat at his heart. And he spoke of filial ingratitude, and said it was all one as if the mouth should tear the hand for lifting food to it; for parents were hands and food and everything to children.

But the good Caius still persisting in his entreaties that the king would not stay out in the open air, at last persuaded him to enter a little wretched hovel which stood upon the heath, where the fool first entering, suddenly ran back terrified, saying that he had seen a spirit. But upon examination this spirit proved to be nothing more than a poor Bedlam beggar, who had crept into this deserted hovel for shelter, and with his talk about devils frighted the fool, one of those poor lunatics who are either mad, or feign to be so, the better to extort charity from the compassionate country people, who go about the country, calling themselves poor Tom and poor Turly-good, saying: 'Who gives anything to poor Tom?' sticking pins and nails and sprigs of rosemary into their arms to make them bleed; and with such horrible actions, partly by prayers, and partly with lunatic curses, they move or terrify the ignorant countryfolks into giving them alms. This poor fellow was such a one; and the king seeing him in so wretched a plight, with nothing but a blanket about his loins to cover his nakedness, could not be persuaded but that the fellow was some father who had given all away to his daughters, and brought himself to that pass:

for nothing he thought could bring a man to such wretchedness but the having unkind daughters.

And from this and many such wild speeches which he uttered, the good Caius plainly perceived that he was not in his perfect mind, but that his daughters' ill usage had really made him go mad. And now the loyalty of this worthy earl of Kent showed itself in more essential services than he had hitherto found opportunity to perform. For with the assistance of some of the king's attendants who remained loyal, he had the person of his royal master removed at daybreak to the castle of Dover, where his own friends and influence, as earl of Kent, chiefly lay; and himself embarking for France, hastened to the court of Cordelia, and did there in such moving terms represent the pitiful condition of her royal father, and set out in such lively colours the inhumanity of her sisters, that this good and loving child with many tears besought the king her husband that he would give her leave to embark for England, with a sufficient power to subdue these cruel daughters and their husbands, and restore the old king her father to his throne; which being granted, she set forth, and with a royal army landed at Dover.

Lear having by some chance escaped from the guardians which the good earl of Kent had put over him to take care of him in his lunacy, was found by some of Cordelia's train, wandering about the fields near Dover, in a pitiable condition, stark mad, and singing aloud to himself with a crown upon his head which he had made of straw, and nettles, and other wild weeds that he had picked up in the corn-fields. By the advice of the physicians, Cordelia, though earnestly desirous of seeing her father, was prevailed upon to put off the meeting, till by sleep and the operation of herbs which they gave him, he should be restored to greater composure. By the aid of these skilful physicians, to whom Cordelia promised all her gold and jewels for the recovery of the old king, Lear was soon in a condition to see his daughter.

A tender sight it was to see the meeting between this

father and daughter; to see the struggles between the joy of this poor old king at beholding again his once darling child, and the shame at receiving such filial kindness from her whom he had cast off for so small a fault in his displeasure; both these passions struggling with the remains of his malady, which in his half-crazed brain sometimes made him that he scarce remembered where he was, or who it was that so kindly kissed him and spoke to him; and then he would beg the standers-by not to laugh at him, if he were mistaken in thinking this lady to be his daughter Cordelia! And then to see him fall on his knees to beg pardon of his child; and she, good lady, kneeling all the while to ask a blessing of him, and telling him that it did not become him to kneel, but it was her duty, for she was his child, his true and very child Cordial! and she kissed him (as she said) to kiss away all her sisters' unkindness, and said that they might be ashamed of themselves, to turn their old kind father with his white beard out into the cold air, when her enemy's dog, though it had bit her (as she prettily expressed it), should have stayed by her fire such a night as that, and warmed himself. And she told her father how she had come from France with purpose to bring him assistance; and he said that she must forget and forgive, for he was old and foolish, and did not know what he did; but that to be sure she had great cause not to love him, but her sisters had none. And Cordelia said that she had no cause, no more than they had.

So we will leave this old king in the protection of his dutiful and loving child, where, by the help of sleep and medicine, she and her physicians at length succeeded in winding up the untuned and jarring senses which the cruelty of his other daughters had so violently shaken. Let us return to say a word or two about those cruel daughters.

These monsters of ingratitude, who had been so false to their old father, could not be expected to prove more faithful to their own husbands. They soon grew tired of paying even the appearance of duty and affection, and in an open way showed they had fixed their loves upon another. It happened that the object of their guilty loves was the same. It was Edmund, a natural son of the late earl of Gloucester, who by his treacheries had succeeded in disinheriting his brother Edgar, the lawful heir, from his earldom, and by his wicked practises was now earl himself; a wicked man, and a fit object for the love of such wicked creatures as Goneril and Regan. It falling out about this time that the duke of Cornwall, Regan's husband, died, Regan immediately declared her intention of wedding this earl of Gloucester, which rousing the jealousy of her sister, to whom as well as to Regan this wicked earl had at sundry times professed love, Goneril found means to make away with her sister by poison; but being detected in her practises, and imprisoned by her husband, the duke of Albany, for this deed, and for her guilty passion for the earl which had come to his ears, she, in a fit of disappointed love and rage, shortly put an end to her own life. Thus the justice of Heaven at last overtook these wicked daughters.

While the eyes of all men were upon this event, admiring the justice displayed in their deserved deaths, the same eyes were suddenly taken off from this sight to admire at the mysterious ways of the same power in the melancholy fate of the young and virtuous daughter, the lady Cordelia, whose good deeds did seem to deserve a more fortunate conclusion: but it is an awful truth, that innocence and piety are not always successful in this world. The forces which Goneril and Regan had sent out under the command of the bad earl of Gloucester were victorious, and Cordelia, by the practises of this wicked earl, who did not like that any should stand between him and the throne, ended her life in prison. Thus, Heaven took this innocent lady to itself in her young years, after showing her to the world an illustrious example of filial duty. Lear did not long survive this kind child.

Before he died, the good earl of Kent, who had still attended his old master's steps from the first of his daughters' ill usage to this sad period of his decay, tried to make him understand that it was he who had followed him under the name of Caius; but Lear's care-crazed brain at that time could not comprehend how that could be, or how Kent and Caius could be the same person: so Kent thought it needless to trouble him with explanations at such a time; and Lear soon after expiring, this faithful servant to the king, between age and grief for his old master's vexations, soon followed him to the grave.

How the judgement of Heaven overtook the bad earl of Gloucester, whose treasons were discovered, and himself slain in single combat with his brother, the lawful earl; and how Goneril's husband, the duke of Albany, who was innocent of the death of Cordelia, and had never encouraged his lady in her wicked proceedings against her father, ascended the throne of Britain after the death of Lear, is needless here to narrate; Lear and his Three Daughters being dead, whose adventures alone concern our story.

MACBETH

When Duncan the Meek reigned king of Scotland, there lived a great thane, or lord, called Macbeth. This Macbeth was a near kinsman to the king, and in great esteem at court for his valour and conduct in the wars; an example of which he had lately given, in defeating a rebel army assisted by the troops of Norway in terrible numbers.

The two Scottish generals, Macbeth and Banquo, returning victorious from this great battle, their way lay over a blasted heath, where they were stopped by the strange appearance of three figures like women, except that they had beards, and their withered skins and wild attire made them look not like any earthly creatures. Macbeth first addressed them, when they, seemingly offended, laid each one her choppy finger upon her skinny lips, in token of silence; and the first of them saluted Macbeth with the title of thane of Glamis. The general was not a little startled to find himself known by such creatures; but how much more, when the second of them followed up that salute by giving him the title of thane of Cawdor, to which honour he had no pretensions; and again the third bid him 'All hail! king that shalt be hereafter!' Such a prophetic greeting might well amaze him, who knew that while the king's sons lived he could not hope to succeed to the throne. Then turning to Banquo, they pronounced him, in a sort of riddling terms, to be *lesser than Macbeth and greater! not so happy, but much happier!* and prophesied that though he should never reign, yet his sons after him should be kings in Scotland. They then turned into air, and vanished: by which the generals knew them to be the weird sisters, or witches.

While they stood pondering on the strangeness of this adventure, there arrived certain messengers from the king, who were empowered by him to confer upon Macbeth the dignity of thane of Cawdor: an event so miraculously corresponding with the prediction of the witches astonished Macbeth, and he stood wrapped in amazement, unable to make reply to the messengers; and in that point of time swelling hopes arose in his mind that the prediction of the third witch might in like manner have its accomplishment, and that he should one day reign king in Scotland.

Turning to Banquo, he said: 'Do you not hope that your children shall be kings, when what the witches promised to me has so wonderfully come to pass?' 'That hope,' answered the general, 'might enkindle you to aim at the throne; but oftentimes these ministers of darkness tell us truths in little things, to betray us into deeds of greatest consequence.'

But the wicked suggestions of the witches had sunk too deep into the mind of Macbeth to allow him to attend to the warnings of the good Banquo. From that time he bent all his thoughts on how to compass the throne of Scotland.

Macbeth had a wife, to whom he communicated the strange prediction of the weird sisters, and its partial accomplishment. She was a bad, ambitious woman, and so as her husband and herself could arrive at greatness, she cared not much by what means. She spurred on the reluctant purpose of Macbeth, who felt compunction at the thoughts of blood, and did not cease to represent the murder of the king as a step absolutely necessary to the fulfilment of the flattering prophecy.

It happened at this time that the king, who out of his royal condescension would oftentimes visit his principal nobility upon gracious terms, came to Macbeth's house, attended by his two sons, Malcolm and Donalbain, and a numerous train of thanes and attendants, the more to honour Macbeth for the triumphal success of his wars.

The castle of Macbeth was pleasantly situated, and the air about it was sweet and wholesome, which appeared by the nests which the martlet, or swallow, had built under all the jutting friezes and buttresses of the building, wherever it found a place of advantage; for where those birds most breed and haunt, the air is observed to be delicate. The king entered well-pleased with the place, and not less so with the attentions and respect of his honoured hostess, lady Macbeth, who had the art of covering treacherous purposes with smiles; and could look like the innocent flower, while she was indeed the serpent under it.

The king being tired with his journey, went early to bed, and in his state-room two grooms of his chamber (as was the custom) slept beside him. He had been unusually pleased with his reception, and had made presents before he retired to his principal officers; and among the rest, had sent a rich diamond to lady Macbeth, greeting her by the name of his most kind hostess.

Now was the middle of night, when over half the world nature seems dead, and wicked dreams abuse men's minds asleep, and none but the wolf and the murderer is abroad. This was the time when lady Macbeth waked to plot the murder of the king. She would not have undertaken a deed so abhorrent to her sex, but that she feared her husband's nature, that it was too full of the milk of human kindness, to do a contrived murder. She knew him to be ambitious, but withal to be scrupulous, and not yet prepared for that height of crime which commonly in the end accompanies inordinate ambition. She had won him to consent to the murder, but she doubted his resolution; and she feared that the natural tenderness of his disposition (more humane than her own) would come between, and defeat the purpose. So with her own hands armed with a dagger, she approached the king's bed; having taken care to ply the grooms of his chamber so with wine, that they slept intoxicated, and careless of their charge.

There lay Duncan in a sound sleep after the fatigues of his journey, and as she viewed him earnestly, there was something in his face, as he slept, which resembled her own father; and she had not the courage to proceed.

She returned to confer with her husband. His resolution had begun to stagger. He considered that there were strong reasons against the deed. In the first place, he was not only a subject, but a near kinsman to the king; and he had been his host and entertainer that day, whose duty, by the laws of hospitality, it was to shut the door against his murderers, not bear the knife himself. Then he considered how just and merciful a king this Duncan had been, how clear of offence to his subjects, how loving to his nobility, and in particular to him; that such kings are the peculiar care of Heaven, and their subjects doubly bound to revenge their deaths. Besides, by the favours of the king, Macbeth stood high in the opinion of all sorts of men, and how would those honours be stained by the reputation of so foul a murder!

In these conflicts of the mind lady Macbeth found her husband inclining to the better part, and resolving to proceed no further. But she being a woman not easily shaken from her evil purpose, began to pour in at his ears words which infused a portion of her own spirit into his mind, assigning reason upon reason why he should not shrink from what he had undertaken; how easy the deed was; how soon it would be over; and how the action of one short night would give to all their nights and days to come sovereign sway and royalty! Then she threw contempt on his change of purpose, and accused him of fickleness and cowardice; and declared that she had given suck, and knew how tender it was to love the babe that milked her; but she would, while it was smiling in her face, have plucked it from her breast, and dashed its brains out, if she had so sworn to do it, as he had sworn to perform that murder. Then she added, how practicable it was to lay the guilt of the deed upon the drunken sleepy grooms. And with the valour of her tongue she so chastised his sluggish resolutions, that he once more summoned up courage to the bloody business.

So, taking the dagger in his hand, he softly stole in the dark to the room where Duncan lay; and as he went, he thought he saw another dagger in the air, with the handle towards him, and on the blade and at the point of it drops of blood; but when he tried to grasp at it, it was nothing but air, a mere phantasm proceeding from his own hot and oppressed brain and the business he had in hand.

Getting rid of this fear, he entered the king's room, whom he despatched with one stroke of his dagger. Just as he had done the murder, one of the grooms, who slept in the chamber, laughed in his sleep, and the other cried: 'Murder,' which woke them both; but they said a short prayer; one of them said: 'God bless us!' and the other answered 'Amen'; and addressed themselves to sleep again. Macbeth, who stood listening to them, tried to say 'Amen,' when the fellow said 'God bless us!' but, though he had most need of a blessing, the word stuck in his throat, and he could not pronounce it.

Again he thought he heard a voice which cried: 'Sleep no more: Macbeth doth murder sleep, the innocent sleep, that nourishes life.' Still it cried: 'Sleep no more,' to all the house. 'Glamis hath murdered sleep, and therefore Cawdor shall sleep no more. Macbeth shall sleep no more.'

With such horrible imaginations Macbeth returned to his listening wife, who began to think he had failed of his purpose, and that the deed was somehow frustrated. He came in so distracted a state, that she reproached him with his want of firmness, and sent him to wash his hands of the blood which stained them, while she took his dagger, with purpose to stain the cheeks of the grooms with blood, to make it seem their guilt.

Morning came, and with it the discovery of the murder, which could not be concealed; and though Macbeth and his lady made great show of grief, and the proofs against the grooms (the dagger being produced against them and their faces smeared with blood) were sufficiently strong,

yet the entire suspicion fell upon Macbeth, whose induce-
ments to such a deed were so much more forcible than
such poor silly grooms could be supposed to have; and
Duncan's two sons fled. Malcolm, the eldest, sought for
refuge in the English court; and the youngest, Donalbain,
made his escape to Ireland.

The king's sons, who should have succeeded him, having thus vacated the throne, Macbeth as next heir was
crowned king, and thus the prediction of the weird sisters
was literally accomplished.

Though placed so high, Macbeth and his queen could
not forget the prophecy of the weird sisters, that, though
Macbeth should be king, yet not his children, but the children of Banquo, should be kings after him. The thought of
this, and that they had defiled their hands with blood, and
done so great crimes, only to place the posterity of Banquo upon the throne, so rankled within them, that they
determined to put to death both Banquo and his son, to
make void the predictions of the weird sisters, which in
their own case had been so remarkably brought to pass.

For this purpose they made a great supper, to which
they invited all the chief thanes; and, among the rest, with
marks of particular respect, Banquo and his son Fleance
were invited. The way by which Banquo was to pass to
the palace at night was beset by murderers appointed by
Macbeth, who stabbed Banquo; but in the scuffle Fleance
escaped. From that Fleance descended a race of monarchs who afterwards filled the Scottish throne, ending
with James the Sixth of Scotland and the First of England,
under whom the two crowns of England and Scotland
were united.

At supper, the queen, whose manners were in the highest degree affable and royal, played the hostess with a
gracefulness and attention which conciliated every one
present, and Macbeth discoursed freely with his thanes
and nobles, saying, that all that was honourable in the
country was under his roof, if he had but his good friend

Banquo present, whom yet he hoped he should rather have to chide for neglect, than to lament for any mischance. Just at these words the ghost of Banquo, whom he had caused to be murdered, entered the room and placed himself on the chair which Macbeth was about to occupy. Though Macbeth was a bold man, and one that could have faced the devil without trembling, at this horrible sight his cheeks turned white with fear, and he stood quite unmanned with his eyes fixed upon the ghost. His queen and all the nobles, who saw nothing but perceived him gazing (as they thought) upon an empty chair, took it for a fit of distraction; and she reproached him, whispering that it was but the same fancy which made him see the dagger in the air, when he was about to kill Duncan. But Macbeth continued to see the ghost, and gave no heed to all they could say, while he addressed it with distracted words, yet so significant, that his queen, fearing the dreadful secret would be disclosed, in great haste dismissed the guests, excusing the infirmity of Macbeth as a disorder he was often troubled with.

To such dreadful fancies Macbeth was subject. His queen and he had their sleeps afflicted with terrible dreams, and the blood of Banquo troubled them not more than the escape of Fleance, whom now they looked upon as father to a line of kings who should keep their posterity out of the throne. With these miserable thoughts they found no peace, and Macbeth determined once more to seek out the weird sisters, and know from them the worst.

He sought them in a cave upon the heath, where they, who knew by foresight of his coming, were engaged in preparing their dreadful charms, by which they conjured up infernal spirits to reveal to them futurity. Their horrid ingredients were toads, bats, and serpents, the eye of a newt, and the tongue of a dog, the leg of a lizard, and the wing of the night-owl, the scale of a dragon, the tooth of a wolf, the maw of the ravenous salt-sea shark, the mummy of a witch, the root of the poisonous hemlock (this to have effect must be digged in the dark), the gall of a goat, and the liver of a Jew, with slips of the yew tree that roots itself in graves, and the finger of a dead child: all these were set on to boil in a great kettle, or cauldron, which, as fast as it grew too hot, was cooled with a baboon's blood: to these they poured in the blood of a sow that had eaten her young, and they threw into the flame the grease that had sweaten from a murderer's gibbet. By these charms they bound the infernal spirits to answer their questions.

It was demanded of Macbeth, whether he would have his doubts resolved by them, or by their masters, the spirits. He, nothing daunted by the dreadful ceremonies which he saw, boldly answered: 'Where are they? let me see them.' And they called the spirits, which were three. And the first arose in the likeness of an armed head, and he called Macbeth by name, and bid him beware of the thane of Fife; for which caution Macbeth thanked him; for Macbeth had entertained a jealousy of Macduff, the thane of Fife.

And the second spirit arose in the likeness of a bloody child, and he called Macbeth by name, and bid him have no fear, but laugh to scorn the power of man, for none of woman born should have power to hurt him; and he advised him to be bloody, bold, and resolute. 'Then live, Macduff!' cried the king; 'what need I fear of thee? but yet I will make assurance doubly sure. Thou shalt not live; that I may tell pale-hearted Fear it lies, and sleep in spite of thunder.'

That spirit being dismissed, a third arose in the form of a child crowned, with a tree in his hand. He called Macbeth by name, and comforted him against conspiracies, saying, that he should never be vanquished, until the wood of Birnam to Dunsinane Hill should come against him. 'Sweet bodements! good!' cried Macbeth; 'who can unfix the forest, and move it from its earth-bound roots? I see I shall live the usual period of man's life, and not be cut off by a violent death. But my heart throbs to know

one thing. Tell me, if your art can tell so much, if Banquo's
issue shall ever reign in this kingdom?' Here the cauldron
sank into the ground, and a noise of music was heard, and
eight shadows, like kings, passed by Macbeth, and Banquo last, who bore a glass which showed the figures of
many more, and Banquo all bloody smiled upon Macbeth,
and pointed to them; by which Macbeth knew that these
were the posterity of Banquo, who should reign after him
in Scotland; and the witches, with a sound of soft music,
and with dancing, making a show of duty and welcome to
Macbeth, vanished. And from this time the thoughts of
Macbeth were all bloody and dreadful.

The first thing he heard when he got out of the witches'
cave, was that Macduff, thane of Fife, had fled to England,
to join the army which was forming against him under
Malcolm, the eldest son of the late king, with intent to dis-
place Macbeth, and set Malcolm, the right heir, upon the
throne. Macbeth, stung with rage, set upon the castle of
Macduff, and put his wife and children, whom the thane
had left behind, to the sword, and extended the slaughter
to all who claimed the least relationship to Macduff.

These and suchlike deeds alienated the minds of all his
chief nobility from him. Such as could, fled to join with
Malcolm and Macduff, who were now approaching with a
powerful army, which they had raised in England; and the
rest secretly wished success to their arms, though for fear
of Macbeth they could take no active part. His recruits
went on slowly. Everybody hated the tyrant; nobody
loved or honoured him; but all suspected him, and he
began to envy the condition of Duncan, whom he had
murdered, who slept soundly in his grave, against whom
treason had done its worst: steel nor poison, domestic
malice nor foreign levies, could hurt him any longer.

While these things were acting, the queen, who had
been the sole partner in his wickedness, in whose bosom
he could sometimes seek a momentary repose from those
terrible dreams which afflicted them both nightly, died, it

is supposed, by her own hands, unable to bear the remorse of guilt, and public hate; by which event he was left alone, without a soul to love or care for him, or a friend to whom he could confide his wicked purposes.

He grew careless of life, and wished for death; but the near approach of Malcolm's army roused in him what remained of his ancient courage, and he determined to die (as he expressed it) 'with armour on his back.' Besides this, the hollow promises of the witches had filled him with a false confidence, and he remembered the sayings of the spirits, that none of woman born was to hurt him, and that he was never to be vanquished till Birnam wood should come to Dunsinane, which he thought could never be. So he shut himself up in his castle, whose impregnable strength was such as defied a siege: here he sullenly waited the approach of Malcolm. When, upon a day, there came a messenger to him, pale and shaking with fear, almost unable to report that which he had seen; for he averred, that as he stood upon his watch on the hill, he looked towards Birnam, and to his thinking the wood began to move! 'Liar and slave!' cried Macbeth: 'if thou speakest false, thou shalt hang alive upon the next tree, till famine end thee. If thy tale be true, I care not if thou dost as much by me': for Macbeth now began to faint in resolution, and to doubt the equivocal speeches of the spirits. He was not to fear till Birnam wood should come to Dunsinane; and now a wood did move! 'However,' said he, 'if this which he avouches be true, let us arm and out. There is no flying hence, nor staying here. I begin to be weary of the sun, and wish my life at an end.' With these desperate speeches he sallied forth upon the besiegers, who had now come up to the castle.

The strange appearance which had given the messenger an idea of a wood moving is easily solved. When the besieging army marched through the wood of Birnam, Malcolm, like a skilful general, instructed his soldiers to hew down every one a bough and bear it before him, by way of concealing the true numbers of his host. This marching of the soldiers with boughs had at a distance the appearance which had frightened the messenger. Thus were the words of the spirit brought to pass, in a sense different from that in which Macbeth had understood them, and one great hold of his confidence was gone.

And now a severe skirmishing took place, in which Macbeth, though feebly supported by those who called themselves his friends, but in reality hated the tyrant and inclined to the party of Malcolm and Macduff, yet fought with the extreme of rage and valour, cutting to pieces all who were opposed to him, till he came to where Macduff was fighting. Seeing Macduff, and remembering the caution of the spirit who had counselled him to avoid Macduff, above all men, he would have turned, but Macduff, who had been seeking him through the whole fight, opposed his turning, and a fierce contest ensued; Macduff giving him many foul reproaches for the murder of his wife and children. Macbeth, whose soul was charged enough with blood of that family already, would still have declined the combat; but Macduff still urged him to it, calling him tyrant, murderer, hell-hound, and villain.

Then Macbeth remembered the words of the spirit, how none of woman born should hurt him; and smiling confidently he said to Macduff: 'Thou losest thy labour, Macduff. As easily thou mayest impress the air with thy sword, as make me vulnerable. I bear a charmed life, which must not yield to one of woman born.'

'Despair thy charm,' said Macduff, 'and let that lying spirit whom thou hast served, tell thee, that Macduff was never born of woman, never as the ordinary manner of men is to be born, but was untimely taken from his mother.'

'Accursed be the tongue which tells me so,' said the trembling Macbeth, who felt his last hold of confidence give way; 'and let never man in future believe the lying equivocations of witches and juggling spirits, who deceive us in words which have double senses, and while they keep their promise literally, disappoint our hopes with a different meaning. I will not fight with thee.'

'Then live!' said the scornful Macduff; 'we will have a show of thee, as men show monsters, and a painted board, on which shall be written: "Here men may see the tyrant!"'

'Never,' said Macbeth, whose courage returned with despair; 'I will not live to kiss the ground before young Malcolm's feet, and to be baited with the curses of the rabble. Though Birnam wood be come to Dunsinane, and thou opposed to me, who wast never born of woman, yet will I try the last.' With these frantic words he threw himself upon Macduff, who, after a severe struggle, in the end overcame him, and cutting off his head, made a present of it to the young and lawful king, Malcolm; who took upon him the government which, by the machinations of the usurper, he had so long been deprived of, and ascended the throne of Duncan the Meek, amid the acclamations of the nobles and the people.

THE TAMING OF THE SHREW

Katharine, the Shrew, was the eldest daughter of Baptista, a rich gentleman of Padua. She was a lady of such an ungovernable spirit and fiery temper, such a loud-tongued scold, that she was known in Padua by no other name than Katharine the Shrew. It seemed very unlikely, indeed impossible, that any gentleman would ever be found who would venture to marry this lady, and therefore Baptista was much blamed for deferring his consent to many excellent offers that were made to her gentle sister Bianca, putting off all Bianca's suitors with this excuse, that when the eldest sister was fairly off his hands, they should have free leave to address young Bianca.

It happened, however, that a gentleman, named Petruchio, came to Padua, purposely to look out for a wife, who, nothing discouraged by these reports of Katharine's temper, and hearing she was rich and handsome, resolved upon marrying this famous termagant, and taming her into a meek and manageable wife. And truly none was so fit to set about this herculean labour as Petruchio, whose spirit was as high as Katharine's, and he was a witty and most happy-tempered humourist, and withal so wise, and of such a true judgement, that he well knew how to feign a passionate and furious deportment, when his spirits were so calm that himself could have laughed merrily at his own angry feigning, for his natural temper was careless and easy; the boisterous airs he assumed when he became the husband of Katharine being but in sport, or more properly speaking, affected by his excellent discernment, as the only means to overcome, in her own way, the passionate ways of the furious Katharine.

A courting then Petruchio went to Katharine the Shrew; and first of all he applied to Baptista her father, for leave to woo his *gentle daughter* Katharine, as Petruchio called her, saying archly, that having heard of her bashful modesty and mild behaviour, he had come from Verona to solicit her love. Her father, though he wished her married, was forced to confess Katharine would ill answer this character, it being soon apparent of what manner of gentleness she was composed, for her music-master rushed into the room to complain that the gentle Katharine, his pupil, had broken his head with her lute, for presuming to find fault with her performance; which, when Petruchio heard, he said: 'It is a brave wench; I love her more than ever, and long to have some chat with her'; and hurrying the old gentleman for a positive answer, he said: 'My business is in haste, signior Baptista, I cannot come every day to woo. You knew my father: he is dead, and has left me heir to all his lands and goods. Then tell me, if I get your daughter's love, what dowry you will give with her.' Baptista thought his manner was somewhat blunt for a lover; but being glad to get Katharine married, he answered that he would give her twenty thousand crowns for her dowry, and half his estate at his death: so this odd match was quickly agreed on, and Baptista went to apprise his shrewish daughter of her lover's addresses, and sent her in to Petruchio to listen to his suit.

In the meantime Petruchio was settling with himself the mode of courtship he should pursue; and he said: 'I will woo her with some spirit when she comes. If she rails at me, why then I will tell her she sings as sweetly as a nightingale; and if she frowns, I will say she looks as clear as roses newly washed with dew. If she will not speak a word, I will praise the eloquence of her language; and if she bids me leave her, I will give her thanks as if she bid me stay with her a week.' Now the stately Katharine entered, and Petruchio first addressed her with 'Good morrow, Kate, for that is your name, I hear.' Katharine, not liking this plain salutation, said disdainfully: 'They call me Katharine who do speak to me.' 'You lie,' replied the lover; 'for you are called plain Kate, and bonny Kate, and sometimes Kate the Shrew: but, Kate, you are the prettiest Kate in Christendom, and therefore, Kate, hearing your mildness praised in every town, I am come to woo you for my wife.'

A strange courtship they made of it. She in loud and angry terms showing him how justly she had gained the name of Shrew, while he still praised her sweet and courteous words, till at length, hearing her father coming, he said (intending to make as quick a wooing as possible): 'Sweet Katharine, let us set this idle chat aside, for your father has consented that you shall be my wife, your dowry is agreed on, and whether you will or no, I will marry you.'

And now Baptista entering, Petruchio told him his daughter had received him kindly, and that she had promised to be married the next Sunday. This Katharine denied, saying she would rather see him hanged on Sunday, and reproached her father for wishing to wed her to such a mad-cap ruffian as Petruchio. Petruchio desired her father not to regard her angry words, for they had agreed she should seem reluctant before him, but that when they were alone he had found her very fond and loving; and he said to her: 'Give me your hand, Kate; I will go to Venice to buy you fine apparel against our wedding day. Provide the feast, father, and bid the wedding guests. I will be sure to bring rings, fine array, and rich clothes, that my Katharine may be fine; and kiss me, Kate, for we will be married on Sunday.'

On the Sunday all the wedding guests were assembled, but they waited long before Petruchio came, and Katharine wept for vexation to think that Petruchio had only been making a jest of her. At last, however, he appeared; but he brought none of the bridal finery he had promised Katharine, nor was he dressed himself like a bridegroom, but in strange disordered attire, as if he meant to make a sport of the serious business he came about; and his servant and the very horses on which they rode were in like manner in mean and fantastic fashion habited.

Petruchio could not be persuaded to change his dress; he said Katharine was to be married to him, and not to his clothes; and finding it was in vain to argue with him, to the church they went, he still behaving in the same mad way, for when the priest asked Petruchio if Katharine should be his wife, he swore so loud that she should, that, all amazed, the priest let fall his book, and as he stooped to take it up, this mad-brained bridegroom gave him such a cuff, that down fell the priest and his book again. And all the while they were being married he stamped and swore so, that the high-spirited Katharine trembled and shook with fear. After the ceremony was over, while they were yet in the church, he called for wine, and drank a loud health to the company, and threw a sop which was at the bottom of the glass full in the sexton's face, giving no other reason for this strange act than that the sexton's beard grew thin and hungerly, and seemed to ask the sop as he was drinking. Never sure was there such a mad marriage; but Petruchio did but put this wildness on, the better to succeed in the plot he had formed to tame his shrewish wife.

Baptista had provided a sumptuous marriage feast, but when they returned from church, Petruchio, taking hold of Katharine, declared his intention of carrying his wife home instantly: and no remonstrance of his father-in-law, or angry words of the enraged Katharine, could make him change his purpose. He claimed a husband's right to dispose of his wife as he pleased, and away he hurried Katharine off: he seeming so daring and resolute that no one dared attempt to stop him.

Petruchio mounted his wife upon a miserable horse, lean and lank, which he had picked out for the purpose,

and himself and his servant no better mounted; they journeyed on through rough and miry ways, and ever when
this horse of Katharine's stumbled, he would storm and
swear at the poor jaded beast, who could scarce crawl
under his burthen, as if he had been the most passionate
man alive.

At length, after a weary journey, during which
Katharine had heard nothing but the wild ravings of
Petruchio at the servant and the horses, they arrived at
his house. Petruchio welcomed her kindly to her home,
but he resolved she should have neither rest nor food
that night. The tables were spread, and supper soon
served; but Petruchio, pretending to find fault with every
dish, threw the meat about the floor, and ordered the servants to remove it away; and all this he did, as he said, in
love for his Katharine, that she might not eat meat that
was not well dressed. And when Katharine, weary and
supperless, retired to rest, he found the same fault with
the bed, throwing the pillows and bedclothes about the
room, so that she was forced to sit down in a chair, where
if she chanced to drop asleep, she was presently awakened by the loud voice of her husband, storming at the
servants for the ill-making of his wife's bridal-bed.

The next day Petruchio pursued the same course, still
speaking kind words to Katharine, but when she attempted
to eat, finding fault with everything that was set before
her, throwing the breakfast on the floor as he had done the
supper; and Katharine, the haughty Katharine, was fain to
beg the servants would bring her secretly a morsel of
food; but they being instructed by Petruchio, replied, they
dared not give her anything unknown to their master. 'Ah,'
said she, 'did he marry me to famish me? Beggars that
come to my father's door have food given them. But I, who
never knew what it was to entreat for anything, am starved
for want of food, giddy for want of sleep, with oaths kept
waking, and with brawling fed; and that which vexes me
more than all, he does it under the name of perfect love,
pretending that if I sleep or eat, it were present death to

me.' Here the soliloquy was interrupted by the entrance
of Petruchio: he, not meaning she should be quite
starved, had brought her a small portion of meat, and he
said to her: 'How fares my sweet Kate? Here, love, you see
how diligent I am, I have dressed your meat myself. I am
sure this kindness merits thanks. What, not a word? Nay,
then you love not the meat, and all the pains I have taken
is to no purpose.' He then ordered the servant to take the
dish away. Extreme hunger, which had abated the pride of
Katharine, made her say, though angered to the heart: 'I
pray you let it stand.' But this was not all Petruchio
intended to bring her to, and he replied: 'The poorest service is repaid with thanks, and so shall mine before you
touch the meat.' On this Katharine brought out a reluctant
'I thank you, sir.' And now he suffered her to make a slender meal, saying: 'Much good may it do your gentle heart,
Kate; eat apace! And now, my honey love, we will return to
your father's house, and revel it as bravely as the best,
with silken coats and caps and golden rings, with ruffs
and scarfs and fans and double change of finery'; and to
make her believe he really intended to give her these gay
things, he called in a tailor and a haberdasher, who
brought some new clothes he had ordered for her, and
then giving her plate to the servant to take away, before
she had half satisfied her hunger, he said: 'What, have you
dined?' The haberdasher presented a cap, saying: 'Here is
the cap your worship bespoke'; on which Petruchio began
to storm afresh, saying the cap was moulded in a por-
ringer, and that it was no bigger than a cockle or walnut
shell, desiring the haberdasher to take it away and make
it bigger. Katharine said: 'I will have this; all gentlewomen
wear such caps as these.' 'When you are gentle,' replied
Petruchio, 'you shall have one too, and not till then.' The
meat Katharine had eaten had a little revived her fallen
spirits, and she said: 'Why, sir, I trust I may have leave to
speak, and speak I will: I am no child, no babe; your bet-
ters have endured to hear me say my mind; and if you cannot, you had better stop your ears.' Petruchio would not

hear these angry words, for he had happily discovered a better way of managing his wife than keeping up a jangling argument with her; therefore his answer was: 'Why, you say true; it is a paltry cap, and I love you for not liking it.' 'Love me, or love me not,' said Katharine, 'I like the cap, and I will have this cap or none.' 'You say you wish to see the gown,' said Petruchio, still affecting to misunderstand her. The tailor then came forward and showed her a fine gown he had made for her. Petruchio, whose intent was that she should have neither cap nor gown, found as much fault with that. 'O mercy, Heaven!' said he, 'what stuff is here! What, do you call this a sleeve? it is like a demi-cannon, carved up and down like an apple tart.' The tailor said: 'You bid me make it according to the fashion of the times'; and Katharine said, she never saw a better fashioned gown. This was enough for Petruchio, and privately desiring these people might be paid for their goods, and excuses made to them for the seemingly strange treatment he bestowed upon them, he with fierce words and furious gestures drove the tailor and the haberdasher out of the room; and then, turning to Katharine, he said: 'Well, come, my Kate, we will go to your father's even in these mean garments we now wear.' And then he ordered his horses, affirming they should reach Baptista's house by dinner-time, for that it was but seven o'clock. Now it was not early morning but the very middle of the day, when he spoke this; therefore Katharine ventured to say, though modestly, being almost overcome by the vehemence of his manner: 'I dare assure you, sir, it is two o'clock, and will be supper-time before we get there.' But Petruchio meant that she should be so completely subdued, that she should assent to everything he said, before he carried her to her father; and therefore, as if he were lord even of the sun, and could command the hours, he said it should be what time he pleased to have it, before he set forward; 'For,' he said, 'whatever I say or do, you still are crossing it. I will not go to-day, and when I go, it shall be what o'clock I say it is.' Another day Katharine

was forced to practise her newly found obedience, and
not till he had brought her proud spirit to such a perfect
subjection, that she dared not remember there was such
a word as contradiction, would Petruchio allow her to go
to her father's house; and even while they were upon their
journey thither, she was in danger of being turned back
again, only because she happened to hint it was the sun,
when he affirmed the moon shone brightly at noonday.
'Now, by my mother's son,' said he, 'and that is myself, it
shall be the moon, or stars, or what I list, before I journey
to your father's house.' He then made as if he were going
back again; but Katharine, no longer Katharine the Shrew,
but the obedient wife, said: 'Let us go forward, I pray, now
we have come so far, and it shall be the sun, or moon, or
what you please, and if you please to call it a rush candle
henceforth, I vowed it shall be so for me.' This he was
resolved to prove, therefore he said again: 'I say, it is the
moon.' 'I know it is the moon,' replied Katharine. 'You lie,
it is the blessed sun,' said Petruchio. 'Then it is the
blessed sun,' replied Katharine; 'but sun it is not, when
you say it is not. What you will have it named, even so it
is, and so it ever shall be for Katharine.' Now then he suffered her to proceed on her journey; but further to try if
this yielding humour would last, he addressed an old gentleman they met on the road as if he had been a young
woman, saying to him: 'Good morrow, gentle mistress';
and asked Katharine if she had ever beheld a fairer gentlewoman, praising the red and white of the old man's
cheeks, and comparing his eyes to two bright stars; and
again he addressed him, saying: 'Fair lovely maid, once
more good day to you!' and said to his wife: 'Sweet Kate,
embrace her for her beauty's sake.' The now completely
vanquished Katharine quickly adopted her husband's
opinion, and made her speech in like sort to the old gentleman, saying to him: 'Young budding virgin, you are fair,
and fresh, and sweet: whither are you going, and where is
your dwelling? Happy are the parents of so fair a child.'
'Why, how now, Kate,' said Petruchio; 'I hope you are not

mad. This is a man, old and wrinkled, faded and withered, and not a maiden, as you say he is.' On this Katharine said: 'Pardon me, old gentleman; the sun has so dazzled my eyes, that everything I look on seemeth green. Now I perceive you are a reverend father: I hope you will pardon me for my sad mistake.' 'Do, good old grandsire,' said Petruchio, 'and tell us which way you are travelling. We shall be glad of your good company, if you are going our way.' The old gentleman replied: ' Fair sir, and you my merry mistress, your strange encounter has much amazed me. My name is Vincentio, and I am going to visit a son of mine who lives at Padua.' Then Petruchio knew the old gentleman to be the father of Lucentio, a young gentleman who was to be married to Baptista's younger daughter, Bianca, and he made Vincentio very happy, by telling him the rich marriage his son was about to make: and they all journeyed on pleasantly together till they came to Baptista's house, where there was a large company assembled to celebrate the wedding of Bianca and Lucentio, Baptista having willingly consented to the marriage of Bianca when he had got Katharine off his hands.

When they entered, Baptista welcomed them to the wedding feast, and there was present also another newly married pair.

Lucentio, Bianca's husband, and Hortensio, the other new married man, could not forbear sly jests, which seemed to hint at the shrewish disposition of Petruchio's wife, and these fond bridegrooms seemed high pleased with the mild tempers of the ladies they had chosen, laughing at Petruchio for his less fortunate choice. Petruchio took little notice of their jokes till the ladies were retired after dinner, and then he perceived Baptista himself joined in the laugh against him: for when Petruchio affirmed that his wife would prove more obedient than theirs, the father of Katharine said: 'Now, in good sadness, son Petruchio, I fear you have got the veriest shrew of all.' 'Well,' said Petruchio, 'I say no, and therefore for assurance that I speak the truth, let us each one send for his wife, and he whose wife is most obedient to come at first when she is sent for, shall win a wager which we will propose.' To this the other two husbands willingly consented, for they were quite confident that their gentle wives would prove more obedient than the headstrong Katharine; and they proposed a wager of twenty crowns, but Petruchio merrily said, he would lay as much as that upon his hawk or hound, but twenty times as much upon his wife. Lucentio and Hortensio raised the wager to a hundred crowns, and Lucentio first sent his servant to desire Bianca would come to him. But the servant returned, and said: 'Sir, my mistress sends you word she is busy and cannot come.' 'How,' said Petruchio, 'does she say she is busy and cannot come? Is that an answer for a wife?' Then they laughed at him, and said, it would be well if Katharine did not send him a worse answer. And now it was Hortensio's turn to send for his wife; and he said to his servant: 'Go, and entreat my wife to come to me.' 'Oh ho! entreat her!' said Petruchio. 'Nay, then, she needs must come.' 'I am afraid, sir,' said Hortensio, 'your wife will not be entreated.' But presently this civil husband looked a little blank, when the servant returned without his mistress; and he said to him: 'How now! Where is my wife?' 'Sir,' said the servant, 'my mistress says, you have some goodly jest in hand, and therefore she will not come. She bids you come to her.' 'Worse and worse!' said Petruchio; and then he sent his servant, saying: 'Sirrah, go to your mistress, and tell her I command her to come to me.' The company had scarcely time to think she would not obey this summons, when Baptista, all in amaze, exclaimed: 'Now, by my *holidame,* here comes Katharine!' and she entered, saying meekly to Petruchio: 'What is your will, sir, that you send for me?' 'Where is your sister and Hortensio's wife?' said he. Katharine replied: 'They sit conferring by the parlour fire.' 'Go, fetch them hither!' said Petruchio. Away went Katharine without reply to perform her husband's command. 'Here is a wonder,' said

Lucentio, 'if you talk of a wonder.' 'And so it is,' said Hortensio; 'I marvel what it bodes.' 'Marry, peace it bodes,' said Petruchio, 'and love, and quiet life, and right supremacy; and, to be short, everything that is sweet and happy.' Katharine's father, overjoyed to see this reformation in his daughter, said: 'Now, fair befall thee, son Petruchio! you have won the wager, and I will add another twenty thousand crowns to her dowry, as if she were another daughter, for she is changed as if she had never been,' 'Nay,' said Petruchio, 'I will win the wager better yet, and show more signs of her new-built virtue and obedience.' Katharine now entering with the two ladies, he continued: 'See where she comes, and brings your froward wives as prisoners to her womanly persuasion. Katharine, that cap of yours does not become you; off with that bauble, and throw it under foot.' Katharine instantly took off her cap, and threw it down. 'Lord!' said Hortensio's wife, 'may I never have a cause to sigh till I am brought to such a silly pass!' And Bianca, she too said: 'Fie, what foolish duty call you this?' On this Bianca's husband said to her: 'I wish your duty were as foolish too! The wisdom of your duty, fair Bianca, has cost me a hundred crowns since dinner- time.' 'The more fool you,' said Bianca, 'for laying on my duty.' 'Katharine,' said Petruchio, 'I charge you tell these headstrong women what duty they owe their lords and husbands.' And to the wonder of all present, the reformed shrewish lady spoke as eloquently in praise of the wife-like duty of obedience, as she had practised it implicitly in a ready submission to Petruchio's will. And Katharine once more became famous in Padua, not as heretofore, as Katharine the Shrew, but as Katharine the most obedient and duteous wife in Padua.

ROMEO AND JULIET

The two chief families in Verona were the rich Capulets and the Montagues. There had been an old quarrel between these families, which was grown to such a height, and so deadly was the enmity between them, that it extended to the remotest kindred, to the followers and retainers of both sides, insomuch that a servant of the house of Montague could not meet a servant of the house of Capulet, nor a Capulet encounter with a Montague by chance, but fierce words and sometimes bloodshed ensued; and frequent were the brawls from such accidental meetings, which disturbed the happy quiet of Verona's streets.

Old lord Capulet made a great supper, to which many fair ladies and many noble guests were invited. All the admired beauties of Verona were present, and all comers were made welcome if they were not of the house of Montague. At this feast of Capulets, Rosaline, beloved of Romeo, son to the old lord Montague, was present; and though it was dangerous for a Montague to be seen in this assembly, yet Benvolio, a friend of Romeo, persuaded the young lord to go to this assembly in the disguise of a mask, that he might see his Rosaline, and seeing her compare her with some choice beauties of Verona, who (he said) would make him think his swan a crow. Romeo had small faith in Benvolio's words; nevertheless, for the love of Rosaline, he was persuaded to go. For Romeo was a sincere and passionate lover, and one that lost his sleep for love, and fled society to be alone, thinking on Rosaline, who disdained him, and never requited his love, with the least show of courtesy or affection; and Benvolio wished to cure his friend of this love by showing him diversity of ladies and company. To this feast of Capulets then young Romeo with Benvolio and their friend Mercutio went masked. Old Capulet bid them welcome, and told them that ladies who had their toes unplagued with corns would dance with them. And the old man was light hearted and merry, and said that he had worn a mask when he was young, and could have told a whispering tale in a fair lady's ear. And they fell to dancing, and Romeo was suddenly struck with the exceeding beauty of a lady who danced there, who seemed to him to teach the torches to burn bright, and her beauty to show by night like a rich jewel worn by a blackamoor; beauty too rich for use, too dear for earth! like a snowy dove trooping with crows (he said), so richly did her beauty and perfections shine above the ladies her companions. While he uttered these praises, he was overheard by Tybalt, a nephew of lord Capulet, who knew him by his voice to be Romeo. And this Tybalt, being of a fiery and passionate temper, could not endure that a Montague should come under cover of a mask, to fleer and scorn (as he said) at their solemnities. And he stormed and raged exceedingly, and would have struck young Romeo dead. But his uncle, the old lord Capulet, would not suffer him to do any injury at that time, both out of respect to his guests, and because Romeo had borne himself like a gentleman, and all tongues in Verona bragged of him to be a virtuous and well-governed youth. Tybalt, forced to be patient against his will, restrained himself, but swore that this vile Montague should at another time dearly pay for his intrusion.

The dancing being done, Romeo watched the place where the lady stood; and under favour of his masking habit, which might seem to excuse in part the liberty, he presumed in the gentlest manner to take her by the hand, calling it a shrine, which if he profaned by touching it, he was a blushing pilgrim, and would kiss it for atonement. 'Good pilgrim,' answered the lady, 'your devotion shows by far too mannerly and too courtly: saints have hands, which pilgrims may touch, but kiss not.' 'Have not saints lips, and pilgrims too?' said Romeo. 'Ay,' said the lady, 'lips which they must use in prayer.' 'O then, my dear saint,' said Romeo, 'hear my prayer, and grant it, lest I despair.' In such like allusions and loving conceits they were engaged, when the lady was called away to her mother. And Romeo inquiring who her mother was, discovered that the lady whose peerless beauty he was so much struck with, was young Juliet, daughter and heir to the lord Capulet, the great enemy of the Montagues; and that he had unknowingly engaged his heart to his foe. This troubled him, but it could not dissuade him from loving. As little rest had Juliet, when she found that the gentleman that she had been talking with was Romeo and a Montague, for she had been suddenly smit with the same hasty and inconsiderate passion for Romeo, which he had conceived for her; and a prodigious birth of love it seemed to her, that she must love her enemy, and that her affections should settle there, where family considerations should induce her chiefly to hate.

It being midnight, Romeo with his companions departed; but they soon missed him, for, unable to stay away from the house where he had left his heart, he leaped the wall of an orchard which was at the back of Juliet's house. Here he had not been long, ruminating on his new love, when Juliet appeared above at a window, through which her exceeding beauty seemed to break like the light of the sun in the east; and the moon, which shone in the orchard with a faint light, appeared to Romeo as if sick and pale with grief at the superior lustre of this new sun. And she, leaning her cheek upon her hand, he passionately wished himself a glove upon that hand, that he might touch her cheek. She all this while thinking herself alone, fetched a deep sigh, and exclaimed: 'Ah me!' Romeo, enraptured to hear her speak, said softly, and unheard by her: 'O speak again, bright angel, for such you appear, being over my head, like a winged messenger from heaven whom mortals fall back to gaze upon.' She, unconscious of being overheard, and full of the new passion which that night's adventure had given birth to, called upon her lover by name (whom she supposed absent): 'O Romeo, Romeo!' said she, 'wherefore art thou Romeo? Deny thy father, and refuse thy name, for my sake; or if thou wilt not, be but my sworn love, and I no longer will be a Capulet.' Romeo, having this encouragement, would fain have spoken, but he was desirous of hearing more; and the lady continued her passionate discourse with herself (as she thought), still chiding Romeo for being Romeo and a Montague, and wishing him some other name, or that he would put away that hated name, and for that name which was no part of himself, he should take all herself. At this loving word Romeo could no longer refrain, but taking up the dialogue as if her words had been addressed to him personally, and not merely in fancy, he bade her call him Love, or by whatever other name she pleased, for he was no longer Romeo, if that name was displeasing to her. Juliet, alarmed to hear a man's voice in the garden, did not at first know who it was, that by favour of the night and darkness had thus stumbled upon the discovery of her secret; but when he spoke again, though her ears had not yet drunk a hundred words of that tongue's uttering, yet so nice is a lover's hearing, that she immediately knew him to be young Romeo, and she expostulated with him on the danger to which he had exposed himself by climbing the orchard walls, for if any of her kinsmen should find him there, it would be death to him, being a Montague. 'Alack,' said Romeo, 'there is more peril in your eye, than in twenty of their swords. Do you but look kind upon me, lady, and I am proof against their enmity. Better my life should be ended by their hate, than that hated life should be prolonged, to live without your love.' 'How came you into this place,' said Juliet, 'and by whose direction?' 'Love directed me,' answered Romeo: 'I am no pilot, yet wert thou as far apart from me, as that vast shore which is washed with the farthest sea, I should venture for such merchandise.' A crimson blush came over Juliet's face, yet unseen by Romeo by reason of the night, when she reflected upon the discovery which she had made, yet not meaning to make it, of her love to Romeo. She would fain have recalled her words, but that was impossible: fain would she have stood upon form, and have kept her lover at a distance, as the custom of discreet ladies is, to frown and be perverse, and give their suitors harsh denials at first; to stand off, and affect a coyness or indifference, where they most love, that their lovers may not think them too lightly or too easily won; for the difficulty of attainment increases the value of the object. But there was no room in her case for denials, or puttings off, or any of the customary arts of delay and protracted courtship. Romeo had heard from her own tongue, when she did not dream that he was near her, a confession of her love. So with an honest frankness, which the novelty of her situation excused, she confirmed the truth of what he had before heard, and addressing him by the name of *fair Montague* (love can sweeten a sour name), she begged him not to impute her easy yielding to levity or an unworthy mind, but that he must lay the fault of it (if it were a fault) upon the accident of the night which had so strangely discovered her thoughts. And she added, that though her behaviour to him might not be sufficiently prudent, measured by the custom of her sex, yet that she would prove more true than many whose prudence was dissembling, and their modesty artificial cunning.

Romeo was beginning to call the heavens to witness, that nothing was farther from his thoughts than to impute a shadow of dishonour to such an honoured lady, when she stopped him, begging him not to swear; for although she joyed in him, yet she had no joy of that night's contract: it was too rash, too unadvised, too sudden. But he being urgent with her to exchange a vow of love with him that night, she said that she already had given him hers before he requested it; meaning, when he overheard her confession; but she would retract what she then bestowed, for the pleasure of giving it again, for her bounty was as infinite as the sea, and her love as deep. From this loving conference she was called away by her nurse, who slept with her, and thought it time for her to be in bed, for it was near to daybreak; but hastily returning, she said three or four words more to Romeo, the purport of which was, that if his love was indeed honourable, and his purpose marriage, she would send a messenger to him tomorrow, to appoint a time for their marriage, when she would lay all her fortunes at his feet, and follow him as her lord through the world. While they were settling this point, Juliet was repeatedly called for by her nurse, and went in and returned, and went and returned again, for she seemed as jealous of Romeo going from her, as a young girl of her bird, which she will let hop a little from her hand, and pluck it back with a silken thread; and Romeo was as loath to part as she; for the sweetest music to lovers is the sound of each other's tongues at night. But at last they parted, wishing mutually sweet sleep and rest for that night.

The day was breaking when they parted, and Romeo, who was too full of thoughts of his mistress and that blessed meeting to allow him to sleep, instead of going home, bent his course to a monastery hard by, to find friar Lawrence. The good friar was already up at his devotions, but seeing young Romeo abroad so early, he conjectured rightly that he had not been abed that night, but that some distemper of youthful affection had kept him waking. He was right in imputing the cause of Romeo's wakefulness to love, but he made a wrong guess at the object, for he thought that his love for Rosaline had kept him waking. But when Romeo revealed his new passion for Juliet, and requested the assistance of the friar to marry them that day, the holy man lifted up his eyes and hands in a sort of wonder at the sudden change in

Romeo's affections, for he had been privy to all Romeo's love for Rosaline, and his many complaints of her disdain: and he said, that young men's love lay not truly in their hearts, but in their eyes. But Romeo replying, that he himself had often chidden him for doting on Rosaline, who could not love him again, whereas Juliet both loved and was beloved by him, the friar assented in some measure to his reasons; and thinking that a matrimonial alliance between young Juliet and Romeo might happily be the means of making up the long breach between the Capulets and the Montagues; which no one more lamented than this good friar, who was a friend to both the families and had often interposed his mediation to make up the quarrel without effect; partly moved by policy, and partly by his fondness for young Romeo, to whom he could deny nothing, the old man consented to join their hands in marriage.

Now was Romeo blessed indeed, and Juliet, who knew his intent from a messenger which she had despatched according to promise, did not fail to be early at the cell of friar Lawrence, where their hands were joined in holy marriage; the good friar praying the heavens to smile upon that act, and in the union of this young Montague and young Capulet to bury the old strife and long dissensions of their families.

The ceremony being over, Juliet hastened home, where she stayed impatient for the coming of night, at which time Romeo promised to come and meet her in the orchard, where they had met the night before; and the time between seemed as tedious to her, as the night before some great festival seems to an impatient child, that has got new finery which it may not put on till the morning.

That same day, about noon, Romeo's friends, Benvolio and Mercutio, walking through the streets of Verona, were met by a party of the Capulets with the impetuous Tybalt at their head. This was the same angry Tybalt who would have fought with Romeo at old lord Capulet's feast. He,

seeing Mercutio, accused him bluntly of associating with
Romeo, a Montague. Mercutio, who had as much fire and
youthful blood in him as Tybalt, replied to this accusation
with some sharpness; and in spite of all Benvolio could
say to moderate their wrath, a quarrel was beginning,
when Romeo himself passing that way, the fierce Tybalt
turned from Mercutio to Romeo, and gave him the disgraceful appellation of villain. Romeo wished to avoid a
quarrel with Tybalt above all men, because he was the
kinsman of Juliet, and much beloved by her; besides, this
young Montague had never thoroughly entered into the
family quarrel, being by nature wise and gentle, and the
name of a Capulet, which was his dear lady's name, was
now rather a charm to allay resentment, than a watch-
word to excite fury. So he tried to reason with Tybalt,
whom he saluted mildly by the name of *good Capulet,* as if
he, though a Montague, had some secret pleasure in uttering that name: but Tybalt, who hated all Montagues as he
hated hell, would hear no reason, but drew his weapon;
and Mercutio, who knew not of Romeo's secret motive for
desiring peace with Tybalt, but looked upon his present
forbearance as a sort of calm dishonourable submission,
with many disdainful words provoked Tybalt to the pros-
ecution of his first quarrel with him; and Tybalt and Mercutio fought, till Mercutio fell, receiving his death's wound
while Romeo and Benvolio were vainly endeavouring to
part the combatants. Mercutio being dead, Romeo kept
his temper no longer, but returned the scornful appellation of villain which Tybalt had given him; and they fought
till Tybalt was slain by Romeo. This deadly broil falling
out in the midst of Verona at noonday, the news of it
quickly brought a crowd of citizens to the spot, and
among them the old lords Capulet and Montague, with
their wives; and soon after arrived the prince himself,
who being related to Mercutio, whom Tybalt had slain,
and having had the peace of his government often disturbed by these brawls of Montagues and Capulets, came
determined to put the law in strictest force against those

who should be found to be offenders. Benvolio, who had been eyewitness to the fray, was commanded by the prince to relate the origin of it; which he did, keeping as near the truth as he could without injury to Romeo, softening and excusing the part which his friends took in it. Lady Capulet, whose extreme grief for the loss of her kinsman Tybalt made her keep no bounds in her revenge, exhorted the prince to do strict justice upon his murderer, and to pay no attention to Benvolio's representation, who, being Romeo's friend and a Montague, spoke partially. Thus she pleaded against her new son-in-law, but she knew not yet that he was her son-in-law and Juliet's husband. On the other hand was to be seen Lady Montague pleading for her child's life, and arguing with some justice that Romeo had done nothing worthy of punishment in taking the life of Tybalt, which was already forfeited to the law by his having slain Mercutio. The prince, unmoved by the passionate exclamations of these women, on a careful examination of the facts, pronounced his sentence, and by that sentence Romeo was banished from Verona.

Heavy news to young Juliet, who had been but a few hours a bride, and now by this decree seemed everlastingly divorced! When the tidings reached her, she at first gave way to rage against Romeo, who had slain her dear cousin: she called him a beautiful tyrant, a fiend angelical, a ravenous dove, a lamb with a wolf's nature, a serpent-heart hid with a flowering face, and other like contradictory names, which denoted the struggles in her mind between her love and her resentment: but in the end love got the mastery, and the tears which she shed for grief that Romeo had slain her cousin, turned to drops of joy that her husband lived whom Tybalt would have slain. Then came fresh tears, and they were altogether of grief for Romeo's banishment. That word was more terrible to her than the death of many Tybalts.

Romeo, after the fray, had taken refuge in friar Lawrence's cell, where he was first made acquainted with the prince's sentence, which seemed to him far more terrible than death. To him it appeared there was no world out of Verona's walls, no living out of the sight of Juliet. Heaven was there where Juliet lived, and all beyond was purgatory, torture, hell. The good friar would have applied the consolation of philosophy to his griefs: but this frantic young man would hear of none, but like a madman he tore his hair, and threw himself all along upon the ground, as he said, to take the measure of his grave. From this unseemly state he was roused by a message from his dear lady, which a little revived him; and then the friar took the advantage to expostulate with him on the unmanly weakness which he had shown. He had slain Tybalt, but would he also slay himself, slay his dear lady, who lived but in his life? The noble form of man, he said, was but a shape of wax, when it wanted the courage which should keep it firm. The law had been lenient to him, that instead of death, which he had incurred, had pronounced by the prince's mouth only banishment. He had slain Tybalt, but Tybalt would have slain him: there was a sort of happiness in that. Juliet was alive, and (beyond all hope) had become his dear wife; therein he was most happy. All these blessings, as the friar made them out to be, did Romeo put from him like a sullen misbehaved wench. And the friar bade him beware, for such as despaired, (he said) died miserable. Then when Romeo was a little calmed, he counselled him that he should go that night and secretly take his leave of Juliet, and thence proceed straitways to Mantua, at which place he should sojourn, till the friar found fit occasion to publish his marriage, which might be a joyful means of reconciling their families; and then he did not doubt but the prince would be moved to pardon him, and he would return with twenty times more joy than he went forth with grief. Romeo was convinced by these wise counsels of the friar, and took his leave to go and seek his lady, proposing to stay with her that night, and by daybreak pursue his journey alone to Mantua; to which place the good friar

promised to send him letters from time to time, acquainting him with the state of affairs at home.

That night Romeo passed with his dear wife, gaining
secret admission to her chamber, from the orchard in
which he had heard her confession of love the night
before. That had been a night of unmixed joy and rapture;
but the pleasures of this night, and the delight which
these lovers took in each other's society, were sadly
allayed with the prospect of parting, and the fatal adventures of the past day. The unwelcome daybreak seemed to
come too soon, and when Juliet heard the morning song
of the lark, she would have persuaded herself that it was
the nightingale, which sings by night; but it was too truly
the lark which sang, and a discordant and unpleasing note
it seemed to her; and the streaks of day in the east too
certainly pointed out that it was time for these lovers to
part. Romeo took his leave of his dear wife with a heavy
heart, promising to write to her from Mantua every hour
in the day; and when he had descended from her chamber-
window, as he stood below her on the ground, in that sad
foreboding state of mind in which she was, he appeared to
her eyes as one dead in the bottom of a tomb. Romeo's
mind misgave him in like manner: but now he was forced
hastily to depart, for it was death for him to be found
within the walls of Verona after daybreak.

This was but the beginning of the tragedy of this pair of
star-crossed lovers. Romeo had not been gone many
days, before the old lord Capulet proposed a match for
Juliet. The husband he had chosen for her, not dreaming
that she was married already, was count Paris, a gallant,
young, and noble gentleman, no unworthy suitor to the
young Juliet, if she had never seen Romeo.

The terrified Juliet was in a sad perplexity at her
father's offer. She pleaded her youth unsuitable to
marriage, the recent death of Tybalt, which had left her
spirits too weak to meet a husband with any face of joy,
and how indecorous it would show for the family of the
Capulets to be celebrating a nuptial feast, when his

funeral solemnities were hardly over: she pleaded every reason against the match, but the true one, namely, that she was married already. But lord Capulet was deaf to all her excuses, and in a peremptory manner ordered her to get ready, for by the following Thursday she should be married to Paris: and having found her a husband, rich, young, and noble, such as the proudest maid in Verona might joyfully accept, he could not bear that out of an affected coyness, as he construed her denial, she should oppose obstacles to her own good fortune.

In this extremity Juliet applied to the friendly friar, always her counsellor in distress, and he asking her if she had resolution to undertake a desperate remedy, and she answering that she would go into the grave alive rather than marry Paris, her own dear husband living; he directed her to go home, and appear merry, and give her consent to marry Paris, according to her father's desire, and on the next night, which was the night before the marriage, to drink off the contents of a phial which he then gave her, the effect of which would be that for two-and-forty hours after drinking it she should appear cold and lifeless; and when the bridegroom came to fetch her in the morning, he would find her to appearance dead; that then she would be borne, as the manner in that country was, uncovered on a bier, to be buried in the family vault; that if she could put off womanish fear, and consent to this terrible trial, in forty-two hours after swallowing the liquid (such was its certain operation) she would be sure to awake, as from a dream; and before she should awake, he would let her husband know their drift, and he should come in the night, and bear her thence to Mantua. Love, and the dread of marrying Paris, gave young Juliet strength to undertake this horrible adventure; and she took the phial of the friar, promising to observe his directions.

Going from the monastery, she met the young count Paris, and modestly dissembling, promised to become his bride. This was joyful news to the lord Capulet and his wife. It seemed to put youth into the old man; and Juliet, who had displeased him exceedingly, by her refusal of the count, was his darling again, now she promised to be obedient. All things in the house were in a bustle against the approaching nuptials. No cost was spared to prepare such festival rejoicings as Verona had never before witnessed.

On the Wednesday night Juliet drank off the potion. She had many misgivings lest the friar, to avoid the blame which might be imputed to him for marrying her to Romeo, had given her poison; but then he was always known for a holy man: then lest she should awake before the time that Romeo was to come for her; whether the terror of the place, a vault of dead Capulets' bones, and where Tybalt, all bloody, lay festering in his shroud, would not be enough to drive her distracted: again she thought of all the stories she had heard of spirits haunting the places where their bodies were bestowed. But then her love for Romeo, and her aversion for Paris returned, and she desperately swallowed the draught, and became insensible.

When young Paris came early in the morning with music to awaken his bride, instead of a living Juliet, her chamber presented the dreary spectacle of a lifeless corpse. What death to his hopes! What confusion then reigned through the whole house! Poor Paris lamenting his bride, whom most detestable death had beguiled him of, had divorced from him even before their hands were joined. But still more piteous it was to hear the mournings of the old lord and lady Capulet, who having but this one, one poor loving child to rejoice and solace in, cruel death had snatched her from their sight, just as these careful parents were on the point of seeing her advanced (as they thought) by a promising and advantageous match. Now all things that were ordained for the festival were turned from their properties to do the office of a black funeral. The wedding cheer served for a sad burial feast, the bridal hymns were changed for sullen dirges, the sprightly instruments to melancholy bells, and the flowers that should have been strewed in the bride's path, now served but to strew her corpse. Now, instead of a priest to marry her, a priest was needed to bury her; and she was borne to church indeed, not to augment the cheerful hopes of the living, but to swell the dreary numbers of the dead.

Bad news, which always travels faster than good, now brought the dismal story of his Juliet's death to Romeo, at Mantua, before the messenger could arrive, who was sent from friar Lawrence to apprise him that these were mock funerals only, and but the shadow and representation of death, and that his dear lady lay in the tomb but for a short while, expecting when Romeo would come to release her from that dreary mansion. Just before, Romeo had been unusually joyful and lighthearted. He had dreamed in the night that he was dead (a strange dream, that gave a dead man leave to think), and that his lady came and found him dead, and breathed such life with kisses in his lips, that he revived, and was an emperor! And now that a messenger came from Verona, he thought surely it was to confirm some good news which his dreams had presaged. But when the contrary to this flattering vision appeared, and that it was his lady who was dead in truth, whom he could not revive by any kisses, he ordered horses to be got ready, for he determined that night to visit Verona, and to see his lady in her tomb. And as mischief is swift to enter into the thoughts of desperate men, he called to mind a poor apothecary, whose shop in Mantua he had lately passed, and from the beggarly appearance of the man, who seemed famished, and the wretched show in his show of empty boxes ranged on dirty shelves, and other tokens of extreme wretchedness, he had said at the time (perhaps having some misgivings that his own disastrous life might haply meet with a conclusion so desperate), 'If a man were to need poison, which by the law of Mantua it is death to sell, here lives a poor wretch who would sell it him.' These words of his now came into his mind, and he sought out the apothecary, who after some pretended scruples, Romeo offering him gold, which his poverty could not resist, sold him a poison, which, if he swallowed, he told him, if he had the strength of twenty men, would quickly despatch him.

With this poison he set out for Verona, to have a sight of his dear lady in her tomb, meaning, when he had satisfied his sight, to swallow the poison, and be buried by her side. He reached Verona at midnight, and found the churchyard, in the midst of which was situated the ancient tomb of the Capulets. He had provided a light, and a spade, and wrenching iron, and was proceeding to break open the monument, when he was interrupted by a voice, which by the name of *vile Montague,* bade him desist from his unlawful business. It was the young count Paris, who had come to the tomb of Juliet at that unseasonable time of night, to strew flowers and to weep over the grave of her that should have been his bride. He knew not what an interest Romeo had in the dead, but knowing him to be a Montague, and (as he supposed) a sworn foe to all the Capulets, he judged that he was come by night to do some villanous shame to the dead bodies; therefore in an angry tone he bade him desist; and as a criminal, condemned by the laws of Verona to die if he were found within the walls of the city, he would have apprehended him. Romeo urged Paris to leave him, and warned him by the fate of Tybalt, who lay buried there, not to provoke his anger, or draw down another sin upon his head, by forcing him to kill him. But the count in scorn refused his warning, and laid hands on him as a felon, which Romeo resisting, they fought, and Paris fell. When Romeo, by the help of a light, came to see who it was that he had slain, that it was Paris, who (he learned in his way from Mantua) should have married Juliet, he took the dead youth by the hand, as one whom misfortune had made a companion, and said that he would bury him in a triumphal grave, meaning in Juliet's grave, which he now opened: and there lay his lady, as one whom death had no power upon to change a feature or complexion, in her matchless beauty; or as if

Death were amorous, and the lean abhorred monster kept
her there for his delight; for she lay yet fresh and bloom-
ing, as she had fallen to sleep when she swallowed that
benumbing potion; and near her lay Tybalt in his bloody
shroud, whom Romeo seeing, begged pardon of his lifeless corpse, and for Juliet's sake called him *cousin,* and
said that he was about to do him a favour by putting his
enemy to death. Here Romeo took his last leave of his
lady's lips, kissing them; and here he shook the burden of
his cross stars from his weary body, swallowing that poison which the apothecary had sold him, whose operation
was fatal and real, not like that dissembling potion which
Juliet had swallowed, the effect of which was now nearly
expiring, and she about to awake to complain that Romeo
had not kept his time, or that he had come too soon.

For now the hour was arrived at which the friar had
promised that she should awake; and he, having learned
that his letters which he had sent to Mantua, by some
unlucky detention of the messenger, had never reached
Romeo, came himself, provided with the pickaxe and
lantern, to deliver the lady from her confinement; but he
was surprised to find a light already burning in the
Capulets' monument, and to see swords and blood near it,
and Romeo and Paris lying breathless by the monument.

Before he could entertain a conjecture, to imagine how
these fatal accidents had fallen out, Juliet awoke out of
her trance, and seeing the friar near her, she remembered
the place where she was, and the occasion of her being
there, and asked for Romeo, but the friar, hearing a noise,
bade her come out of that place of death, and of unnatural
sleep, for a greater power than they could contradict had
thwarted their intents; and being frightened by the noise
of people coming, he fled: but when Juliet saw the cup
closed in her true love's hand, she guessed that poison
had been the cause of his end, and she would have swallowed the dregs if any had been left, and she kissed his
still warm lips to try if any poison yet did hang upon

them; then hearing a nearer noise of people coming, she quickly unsheathed a dagger which she wore, and stabbing herself, died by her true Romeo's side.

The watch by this time had come up to the place. A page belonging to count Paris, who had witnessed the fight between his master and Romeo, had given the alarm, which had spread among the citizens, who went up and down the streets of Verona confusedly exclaiming, A Paris! a Romeo! a Juliet! as the rumour had imperfectly reached them, till the uproar brought lord Montague and lord Capulet out of their beds, with the prince, to inquire into the causes of the disturbance. The friar had been apprehended by some of the watch, coming from the churchyard, trembling, sighing, and weeping, in a suspicious manner. A great multitude being assembled at the Capulets' monument, the friar was demanded by the prince to deliver what he knew of these strange and disastrous accidents.

And there, in the presence of the old lords Montague and Capulet, he faithfully related the story of their children's fatal love, the part he took in promoting their marriage, in the hope in that union to end the long quarrels between their families: how Romeo, there dead, was husband to Juliet; and Juliet, there dead, was Romeo's faithful wife; how before he could find a fit opportunity to divulge their marriage, another match was projected for Juliet, who, to avoid the crime of a second marriage, swallowed the sleeping draught (as he advised), and all thought her dead; how meantime he wrote to Romeo, to come and take her thence when the force of the potion should cease, and by what unfortunate miscarriage of the messenger the letters never reached Romeo; further than this the friar could not follow the story, nor knew more than that coming himself, to deliver Juliet from that place of death, he found the count Paris and Romeo slain. The remainder of the transactions was supplied by the narration of the page who had seen Paris and Romeo fight, and by the servant who came with Romeo from Verona, to whom this faithful lover had given letters to be delivered to his father in the event of his death, which made good the friar's words, confessing his marriage with Juliet, imploring the forgiveness of his parents, acknowledging the buying of the poison of the poor apothecary, and his intent in coming to the monument, to die, and lie with Juliet. All these circumstances agreed together to clear the friar from any hand he could be supposed to have in these complicated slaughters, further than as the unintended consequences of his own well meant, yet too artificial and subtle contrivances.

And the prince, turning to these old lords, Montague and Capulet, rebuked them for their brutal and irrational enmities, and showed them what a scourge Heaven had laid upon such offences, that it had found means even through the love of their children to punish their unnatural hate. And these old rivals, no longer enemies, agreed to bury their long strife in their children's graves; and lord Capulet requested lord Montague to give him his hand, calling him by the name of brother, as if in acknowledgement of the union of their families, by the marriage of the young Capulet and Montague; and saying that lord Montague's hand (in token of reconcilement) was all he demanded for his daughter's jointure: but lord Montague said he would give him more, for he would raise her a statue of pure gold, that while Verona kept its name, no figure should be so esteemed for its richness and workmanship as that of the true and faithful Juliet. And lord Capulet in return said that he would raise another statue to Romeo. So did these poor old lords, when it was too late, strive to outdo each other in mutual courtesies: while so deadly had been their rage and enmity in past times, that nothing but the fearful overthrow of their children (poor sacrifices to their quarrels and dissensions) could remove the rooted hates and jealousies of the noble families.

HAMLET, PRINCE OF DENMARK

Gertrude, queen of Denmark, becoming a widow by the sudden death of King Hamlet, in less than two months after his death married his brother Claudius, which was noted by all people at the time for a strange act of indiscretion, or unfeelingness, or worse: for this Claudius did no ways resemble her late husband in the qualities of his person or his mind, but was as contemptible in outward appearance, as he was base and unworthy in disposition; and suspicions did not fail to arise in the minds of some, that he had privately made away with his brother, the late king, with the view of marrying his widow, and ascending the throne of Denmark, to the exclusion of young Hamlet, the son of the buried king, and lawful successor to the throne.

But upon no one did this unadvised action of the queen make such impression as upon this young prince, who loved and venerated the memory of his dead father almost to idolatry, and being of a nice sense of honour, and a most exquisite practiser of propriety himself, did sorely take to heart this unworthy conduct of his mother Gertrude: insomuch that, between grief for his father's death and shame for his mother's marriage, this young prince was overclouded with a deep melancholy, and lost all his mirth and all his good looks; all his customary pleasure in books forsook him, his princely exercises and sports, proper to his youth, were no longer acceptable; he grew weary of the world, which seemed to him an unweeded garden, where all the wholesome flowers were choked up, and nothing but weeds could thrive. Not that the prospect of exclusion from the throne, his lawful inheritance, weighed so much upon his spirits, though that to a young and high-minded prince was a bitter wound and a sore indignity; but what so galled him, and took away all his cheerful spirits, was, that his mother had shown herself so forgetful to his father's memory; and such a father! who had been to her so loving and so gentle a husband! and then she always appeared as loving and obedient a wife to him, and would hang upon him as if her affection grew to him: and now within two months, or as it seemed to young Hamlet, less than two months, she had married again, married his uncle, her dear husband's brother, in itself a highly improper and unlawful marriage, from the nearness of relationship, but made much more so by the indecent haste with which it was concluded, and the unkingly character of the man whom she had chosen to be the partner of her throne and bed. This it was, which more than the loss of ten kingdoms, dashed the spirits and brought a cloud over the mind of this honourable young prince.

In vain was all that his mother Gertrude or the king could do to contrive to divert him; he still appeared in court in a suit of deep black, as mourning for the king his father's death, which mode of dress he had never laid aside, not even in compliment to his mother upon the day she was married, nor could he be brought to join in any of the festivities or rejoicings of that (as appeared to him) disgraceful day.

What mostly troubled him was an uncertainty about the manner of his father's death. It was given out by Claudius that a serpent had stung him; but young Hamlet had shrewd suspicions that Claudius himself was the serpent; in plain English, that he had murdered him for his crown, and that the serpent who stung his father did now sit on the throne.

How far he was right in this conjecture, and what he

ought to think of his mother, how far she was privy to this murder, and whether by her consent or knowledge, or without, it came to pass, were the doubts which continually harassed and distracted him.

A rumour had reached the ear of young Hamlet, that an apparition, exactly resembling the dead king his father, had been seen by the soldiers upon watch, on the platform before the palace at midnight, for two or three nights successively. The figure came constantly clad in the same suit of armour, from head to foot, which the dead king was known to have worn: and they who saw it (Hamlet's bosom friend Horatio was one) agreed in their testimony as to the time and manner of its appearance: that it came just as the clock struck twelve; that it looked pale, with a face more of sorrow than of anger; that its beard was grisly, and the colour a *sable silvered,* as they had seen it in his lifetime: that it made no answer when they spoke to it; yet once they thought it lifted up its head, and addressed itself to motion, as if it were about to speak; but in that moment the morning cock crew, and it shrunk in haste away, and vanished out of their sight.

The young prince, strangely amazed at their relation, which was too consistent and agreeing with itself to disbelieve, concluded that it was his father's ghost which they had seen, and determined to take his watch with the soldiers that night, that he might have a chance of seeing it; for he reasoned with himself, that such an appearance did not come for nothing, but that the ghost had something to impart, and though it had been silent hitherto, yet it would speak to him. And he waited with impatience for the coming of night.

When night came he took his stand with Horatio, and Marcellus, one of the guard, upon the platform, where this apparition was accustomed to walk: and it being a cold night, and the air unusually raw and nipping, Hamlet and Horatio and their companion fell into some talk about the coldness of the night, which was suddenly broken off by Horatio announcing that the ghost was coming.

At the sight of his father's spirit, Hamlet was struck with a sudden surprise and fear. He at first called upon the angels and heavenly ministers to defend them, for he knew not whether it were a good spirit or bad; whether it came for good or evil: but he gradually assumed more courage; and his father (as it seemed to him) looked upon him so piteously, and as it were desiring to have conversation with him, and did in all respects appear so like himself as he was when he lived, that Hamlet could not help addressing him: he called him by his name, Hamlet, King, Father! and conjured him that he would tell the reason why he had left his grave, where they had seen him quietly bestowed, to come again and visit the earth and the moonlight: and besought him that he would let them know if there was anything which they could do to give peace to his spirit. And the ghost beckoned to Hamlet, that he should go with him to some more removed place, where they might be alone; and Horatio and Marcellus would have dissuaded the young prince from following it, for they feared lest it should be some evil spirit, who would tempt him to the neighbouring sea, or to the top of some dreadful cliff, and there put on some horrible shape which might deprive the prince of his reason. But their counsels and entreaties could not alter Hamlet's determination, who cared too little about life to fear the losing of it; and as to his soul, he said, what could the spirit do to that, being a thing immortal as itself? And he felt as hardy as a lion, and bursting from them, who did all they could to hold him, he followed whithersoever the spirit led him.

And when they were alone together, the spirit broke silence, and told him that he was the ghost of Hamlet, his father, who had been cruelly murdered, and he told the manner of it; that it was done by his own brother Claudius, Hamlet's uncle, as Hamlet had already but too much suspected, for the hope of succeeding to his bed and crown. That as he was sleeping in his garden, his custom always in the afternoon, his treasonous brother stole upon him in his sleep, and poured the juice of poisonous henbane into his ears, which has such an antipathy to the life of man, that swift as quicksilver it courses through all the veins of the body, baking up the blood, and spreading a crustlike leprosy all over the skin: thus sleeping, by a brother's hand he was cut off at once from his crown, his queen, and his life: and he adjured Hamlet, if he did ever his dear father love, that he would revenge his foul murder. And the ghost lamented to his son, that his mother should so fall off from virtue, as to prove false to the wedded love of her first husband, and to marry his murderer; but he cautioned Hamlet, howsoever he proceeded in his revenge against his wicked uncle, by no means to act any violence against the person of his mother, but to leave her to heaven, and to the stings and thorns of conscience. And Hamlet promised to observe the ghost's direction in all things, and the ghost vanished.

And when Hamlet was left alone, he took up a solemn resolution, that all he had in his memory, all that he had ever learned by books or observation, should be instantly forgotten by him, and nothing live in his brain but the memory of what the ghost had told him, and enjoined him to do. And Hamlet related the particulars of the conversation which had passed to none but his dear friend Horatio; and he enjoined both to him and Marcellus the strictest secrecy as to what they had seen that night.

The terror which the sight of the ghost had left upon the senses of Hamlet, he being weak and dispirited before, almost unhinged his mind, and drove him beside his reason. And he, fearing that it would continue to have this effect, which might subject him to observation, and set his uncle upon his guard, if he suspected that he was meditating anything against him, or that Hamlet really knew more of his father's death than he professed, took up a strange resolution, from that time to counterfeit as if he were really and truly mad; thinking that he would be less an object of suspicion when his uncle should believe him incapable of any serious project, and that his real perturbation of mind would be best covered and pass concealed under a disguise of pretended lunacy.

From this time Hamlet affected a certain wildness and strangeness in his apparel, his speech, and behaviour, and did so excellently counterfeit the madman, that the king and queen were both deceived, and not thinking his grief for his father's death a sufficient cause to produce such a distemper, for they knew not of the appearance of the ghost, they concluded that his malady was love, and they thought they had found out the object.

Before Hamlet fell into the melancholy way which has been related, he had dearly loved a fair maid called Ophelia, the daughter of Polonius, the king's chief counsellor in affairs of state. He had sent her letters and rings, and made many tenders of his affection to her, and importuned her with love in honourable fashion: and she had given belief to his vows and importunities. But the melancholy which he fell into latterly had made him neglect her, and from the time he conceived the project of counterfeiting madness, he affected to treat her with unkindness, and a sort of rudeness: but she good lady, rather than reproach him with being false to her, persuaded herself that it was nothing but the disease in his mind, and no settled unkindness, which had made him less observant of her than formerly; and she compared the faculties of his once noble mind and excellent understanding, impaired as they were with the deep melancholy that oppressed him, to sweet bells which in themselves are capable of most exquisite music, but when jangled out of tune, or rudely handled, produce only a harsh and unpleasing sound.

Though the rough business which Hamlet had in hand, the revenging of his father's death upon his murderer, did not suit with the playful state of courtship, or admit of the society of so idle a passion as love now seemed to him, yet it could not hinder but that soft thoughts of his Ophelia would come between, and in one of these moments, when he thought that his treatment of this gentle lady had been unreasonably harsh, he wrote her a letter full of wild starts of passion, and in extravagant terms, such as agreed with his supposed madness, but mixed with some

gentle touches of affection, which could not but show to
this honoured lady that a deep love for her yet lay at the
bottom of his heart. He bade her to doubt the stars were
fire, and to doubt that the sun did move, to doubt truth to
be a liar, but never to doubt that he loved; with more of
such extravagant phrases. This letter Ophelia dutifully
showed to her father, and the old man thought himself
bound to communicate it to the king and queen, who from
that time supposed that the true cause of Hamlet's madness was love. And the queen wished that the good beauties of Ophelia might be the happy cause of his wildness,
for so she hoped that her virtues might happily restore
him to his accustomed way again, to both their honours.

But Hamlet's malady lay deeper than she supposed, or
than could be so cured. His father's ghost, which he had
seen, still haunted his imagination, and the sacred injunction to revenge his murder gave him no rest till it was
accomplished. Every hour of delay seemed to him a sin,
and a violation of his father's commands. Yet how to compass the death of the king, surrounded as he constantly
was with his guards, was no easy matter. Or if it had been,
the presence of the queen, Hamlet's mother, who was gen-
erally with the king, was a restraint upon his purpose,
which he could not break through. Besides, the very cir-
cumstance that the usurper was his mother's husband
filled him with some remorse, and still blunted the edge of
his purpose. The mere act of putting a fellow-creature to
death was in itself odious and terrible to a disposition naturally so gentle as Hamlet's was. His very melancholy, and
the dejection of spirits he had so long been in, produced
an irresoluteness and wavering of purpose, which kept
him from proceeding to extremities. Moreover, he could
not help having some scruples upon his mind, whether
the spirit which he had seen was indeed his father, or
whether it might not be the devil, who he had heard has
power to take any form he pleases, and who might have
assumed his father's shape only to take advantage of his
weakness and his melancholy, to drive him to the doing of

so desperate an act as murder. And he determined that he would have more certain grounds to go upon than a vision, or apparition, which might be a delusion.

While he was in this irresolute mind there came to the court certain players, in whom Hamlet formerly used to take delight, and particularly to hear one of them speak a tragical speech, describing the death of old Priam, King of Troy, with the grief of Hecuba his queen. Hamlet welcomed his old friends, the players, and remembering how that speech had formerly given him pleasure, requested the player to repeat it; which he did in so lively a manner, setting forth the cruel murder of the feeble old king, with the destruction of his people and city by fire, and the mad grief of the old queen, running barefoot up and down the palace, with a poor clout upon that head where a crown had been, and with nothing but a blanket upon her loins, snatched up in haste, where she had worn a royal robe; that not only it drew tears from all that stood by, who thought they saw the real scene, so lively was it represented, but even the player himself delivered it with a broken voice and real tears. This put Hamlet upon thinking, if that player could so work himself up to passion by a mere fictitious speech, to weep for one that he had never seen, for Hecuba, that had been dead so many hundred years, how dull was he, who having a read motive and cue for passion, a real king and a dear father murdered, was yet so little moved, that his revenge all this while had seemed to have slept in dull and muddy forgetfulness! and while he meditated on actors and acting, and the powerful effects which a good play, represented to the life, has upon the spectator, he remembered the instance of some murderer, who seeing a murder on the stage, was by the mere force of the scene and resemblance of circumstances so affected, that on the spot he confessed the crime which he had committed. And he determined that these players should play something like the murder of his father before his uncle, and he would watch narrowly what effect it might have upon him, and from his looks he would be able to gather with more certainty if he were the murderer or not. To this effect he ordered a play to be prepared, to the representation of which he invited the king and queen.

The story of the play was of a murder done in Vienna upon a duke. The duke's name was Gonzago, his wife Baptista. The play showed how one Lucianus, a near relation to the duke, poisoned him in his garden for his estate, and how the murderer in a short time after got the love of Gonzago's wife.

At the representation of this play, the king, who did not know the trap which was laid for him, was present, with his queen and the whole court: Hamlet sitting attentively near him to observe his looks. The play began with a conversation between Gonzago and his wife, in which the lady made many protestations of love, and of never marrying a second husband, if she should outlive Gonzago; wishing she might be accursed if she ever took a second husband, and adding that no woman did so, but those wicked women who kill their first husbands. Hamlet observed the king his uncle change colour at this expression, and that it was as bad as wormwood both to him and to the queen. But when Lucianus, according to the story, came to poison Gonzago sleeping in the garden, the strong resemblance which it bore to his own wicked act upon the late king, his brother, whom he had poisoned in his garden, so struck upon the conscience of this usurper, that he was unable to sit out the rest of the play, but on a sudden calling for lights to his chamber, and affecting or partly feeling a sudden sickness, he abruptly left the theatre. The king being departed, the play was given over. Now Hamlet had seen enough to be satisfied that the words of the ghost were true, and no illusion; and in a fit of gaiety, like that which comes over a man who suddenly has some great doubt or scruple resolved, he swore to Horatio, that he would take the ghost's word for a thousand pounds. But before he could make up his resolution as to what measures of revenge he should take, now he was certainly informed that his uncle was his father's murderer, he was sent for by the queen his mother, to a private conference in her closet.

It was by desire of the king that the queen sent for Hamlet, that she might signify to her son how much his late behaviour had displeased them both, and the king, wishing to know all that passed at that conference, and thinking that the too partial report of a mother might let slip some part of Hamlet's words, which it might much import the king to know, Polonius, the old counsellor of state, was ordered to plant himself behind the hangings in the queen's closet, where he might unseen hear all that passed. This artifice was particularly adapted to the disposition of Polonius, who was a man grown old in crooked maxims and policies of state, and delighted to get at the knowledge of matters in an indirect and cunning way.

Hamlet being come to his mother, she began to tax him in the roundest way with his actions and behaviour, and she told him that he had given great offence to *his father,* meaning the king, his uncle, whom, because he had married her, she called Hamlet's father. Hamlet, sorely indignant that she should give so dear and honoured a name as father seemed to him, to a wretch who was indeed no better than the murderer of his true father, with some sharpness replied: 'Mother, *you* have much offended *my father.*' The queen said that was but an idle answer. 'As good as the question deserved,' said Hamlet. The queen asked him if he had forgotten who it was he was speaking to? 'Alas!' replied Hamlet, 'I wish I could forget. You are the queen, your husband's brother's wife; and you are my mother: I wish you were not what you are.' 'Nay; then,' said the queen, 'if you show me so little respect, I will set those to you that can speak,' and was going to send the king or Polonius to him. But Hamlet would not let her go, now he had her alone, till he had tried if his words could not bring her to some sense of her wicked life; and, taking her by the wrist, he held her fast, and made her sit down. She, affrighted at his earnest manner, and fearful lest in

his lunacy he should do her a mischief, cried out; and a
voice was heard from behind the hangings: 'Help, help,
the queen!' which Hamlet hearing, and verily thinking that
it was the king himself there concealed, he drew his sword
and stabbed at the place where the voice came from, as
he would have stabbed a rat that ran there, till the voice
ceasing, he concluded the person to be dead. But when he
dragged for the body, it was not the king, but Polonius,
the old officious counsellor, that had planted himself as a
spy behind the hangings. 'Oh me!' exclaimed the queen,
'what a rash and bloody deed have you done!' 'A bloody
deed, mother,' replied Hamlet, 'but not so bad as yours,
who killed a king, and married his brother.' Hamlet had
gone too far to leave off here. He was now in the humour
to speak plainly to his mother, and he pursued it. And
though the faults of parents are to be tenderly treated by
their children, yet in the case of great crimes the son may
have leave to speak even to his own mother with some
harshness, so as that harshness is meant for her good,
and to turn her from her wicked ways, and not done for
the purpose of upbraiding. And now this virtuous prince
did in moving terms represent to the queen the heinous-
ness of her offence, in being so forgetful of the dead king,
his father, as in so short a space of time to marry with his
brother and reputed murderer: such an act as, after the
vows which she had sworn to her first husband, was
enough to make all vows of women suspected, and all
virtue to be accounted hypocrisy, wedding contracts to
be less than gamesters' oaths, and religion to be a mock-
ery and a mere form of words. He said she had done such
a deed, that the heavens blushed at it, and the earth was
sick of her because of it. And he showed her two pictures,
the one of the late king, her first husband, and the other
of the present king, her second husband, and he bade her
mark the difference; what a grace was on the brow of his
father, how like a god he looked! the curls of Apollo, the
forehead of Jupiter, the eye of Mars, and a posture like to
Mercury newly alighted on some heaven-kissing hill! this

man, he said, *had been* her husband. And then he showed
her whom she had got in his stead: how like a blight or a
mildew he looked, for so he had blasted his wholesome
brother. And the queen was sore ashamed that he should
so turn her eyes inward upon her soul, which she now saw
so black and deformed. And he asked her how she could
continue to live with this man, and be a wife to him, who
had murdered her first husband, and got the crown by as
false means as a thief—and just as he spoke, the ghost of
his father, such as he was in his lifetime, and such as he
had lately seen it, entered the room, and Hamlet, in great
terror, asked what it would have; and the ghost said that it
came to remind him of the revenge he had promised,
which Hamlet seemed to have forgot; and the ghost bade
him speak to his mother, for the grief and terror she was in
would else kill her. It then vanished, and was seen by none
but Hamlet, neither could he by pointing to where it stood,
or by any description, make his mother perceive it; who
was terribly frightened all this while to hear him convers-
ing, as it seemed to her, with nothing; and she imputed it
to the disorder of his mind. But Hamlet begged her not to
flatter her wicked soul in such a manner as to think that it
was his madness, and not her own offences, which had
brought his father's spirit again on the earth. And he bade
her feel his pulse, how temperately it beat, not like a madman's. And he begged of her with tears, to confess herself
to heaven for what was past, and for the future to avoid
the company of the king, and be no more as a wife to him:
and when she should show herself a mother to him, by
respecting his father's memory, he would ask a blessing of
her as a son. And she promising to observe his directions,
the conference ended.

And now Hamlet was at leisure to consider who it was
that in his unfortunate rashness he had killed: and when
he came to see that it was Polonius, the father of the lady
Ophelia, whom he so dearly loved, he drew apart the
dead body, and, his spirits being now a little quieter, he
wept for what he had done.

The unfortunate death of Polonius gave the king a pretence for sending Hamlet out of the kingdom. He would willingly have put him to death, fearing him as dangerous; but he dreaded the people, who loved Hamlet, and the queen who, with all her faults, doted upon the prince, her son. So this subtle king, under pretence of providing for Hamlet's safety, that he might not be called to account for Polonius' death, caused him to be conveyed on board a ship bound for England, under the care of two courtiers, by whom he despatched letters to the English court, which in that time was in subjection and paid tribute to Denmark, requiring for special reasons there pretended, that Hamlet should be put to death as soon as he landed on English ground. Hamlet, suspecting some treachery, in the night-time secretly got at the letters, and skilfully erasing his own name, he in the stead of it put in the names of those two courtiers, who had the charge of him, to be put to death: then sealing up the letters, he put them into their place again. Soon after the ship was attacked by pirates, and a sea-fight commenced; in the course of which Hamlet, desirous to show his valour, with sword in hand singly boarded the enemy's vessel; while his own ship, in a cowardly manner, bore away, and leaving him to his fate, the two courtiers made the best of their way to England, charged with those letters the sense of which Hamlet had altered to their own deserved destruction.

The pirates, who had the prince in their power, showed themselves gentle enemies; and knowing whom they had got prisoner, in the hope that the prince might do them a good turn at court in recompense for any favour they might show him, they set Hamlet on shore at the nearest port in Denmark. From that place Hamlet wrote to the king, acquainting him with the strange chance which had brought him back to his own country, and saying that on the next day he should present himself before his majesty. When he got home, a sad spectacle offered itself the first thing to his eyes.

This was the funeral of the young and beautiful Ophelia,

his once dear mistress. The wits of this young lady had begun to turn ever since her poor father's death. That he should die a violent death, and by the hands of the prince whom she loved, so affected this tender young maid, that in a little time she grew perfectly distracted, and would go about giving flowers away to the ladies of the court, and saying that they were for her father's burial, singing songs about love and about death, and sometimes such as had no meaning at all, as if she had no memory of what happened to her. There was a willow which grew slanting over a brook, and reflected its leaves on the stream. To this brook she came one day when she was unwatched, with garlands she had been making, mixed up of daisies and nettles, flowers and weeds together, and clambering up to hang her garland upon the boughs of the willow, a bough broke, and precipitated this fair young maid, garland, and all that she had gathered, into the water, where her clothes bore her up for a while, during which she chanted scraps of old tunes, like one insensible to her own distress, or as if she were a creature natural to that element: but long it was not before her garments, heavy with the wet, pulled her in from her melodious singing to a muddy and miserable death. It was the funeral of this fair maid which her brother Laertes was celebrating, the king and queen and whole court being present, when Hamlet arrived. He knew not what all this show imported, but stood on one side, not inclining to interrupt the ceremony. He saw the flowers strewed upon her grave, as the custom was in maiden burials, which the queen herself threw in; and as she threw them she said: 'Sweets to the sweet! I thought to have decked thy bride-bed, sweet maid, not to have strewed thy grave. Thou shouldst have been my Hamlet's wife.' And he heard her brother wish that violets might spring from her grave: and he saw him leap into the grave all frantic with grief, and bid the attendants pile mountains of earth upon him, that he might be buried with her. And Hamlet's love for this fair maid came back to him, and he could not bear that a brother should show so much transport of grief, for he thought that he loved Ophelia better than forty thousand brothers. Then discovering himself, he leaped into the grave where Laertes was, all as frantic or more frantic than he, and Laertes knowing him to be Hamlet, who had been the cause of his father's and his sister's death, grappled him by the throat as an enemy, till the attendants parted them: and Hamlet, after the funeral, excused his hasty act in throwing himself into the grave as if to brave Laertes; but he said he could not bear that any one should seem to outgo him in grief for the death of the fair Ophelia. And for the time these two noble youths seemed reconciled.

But out of the grief and anger of Laertes for the death of his father and Ophelia, the king, Hamlet's wicked uncle, contrived destruction for Hamlet. He set on Laertes, under cover of peace and reconciliation, to challenge Hamlet to a friendly trial of skill at fencing, which Hamlet accepting, a day was appointed to try the match. At this match all the court was present, and Laertes, by direction of the king, prepared a poisoned weapon. Upon this match great wagers were laid by the courtiers, as both Hamlet and Laertes were known to excel at this sword play; and Hamlet taking up the foils chose one, not at all suspecting the treachery of Laertes, or being careful to examine Laertes' weapon, who, instead of a foil or blunted sword, which the laws of fencing require, made use of one with a point, and poisoned. At first Laertes did but play with Hamlet, and suffered him to gain some advantages, which the dissembling king magnified and extolled beyond measure, drinking to Hamlet's success, and wagering rich bets upon the issue: but after a few passes, Laertes growing warm made a deadly thrust at Hamlet with his poisoned weapon, and gave him a mortal blow. Hamlet incensed, but not knowing the whole of the treachery, in the scuffle exchanged his own innocent weapon for Laertes' deadly one, and with a thrust of Laertes' own sword repaid Laertes home, who was thus justly caught in his own treachery. In this instant the

queen shrieked out that she was poisoned. She had inad-
vertently drunk out of a bowl which the king had prepared for Hamlet, in case, that being warm in fencing, he
should call for drink: into this the treacherous king had
infused a deadly poison, to make sure of Hamlet, if Laertes
had failed. He had forgotten to warn the queen of the
bowl, which she drank of, and immediately died, exclaiming with her last breath that she was poisoned. Hamlet,
suspecting some treachery, ordered the doors to be shut,
while he sought it out. Laertes told him to seek no farther,
for he was the traitor; and feeling his life go away with the
wound which Hamlet had given him, he made confession
of the treachery he had used, and now he had fallen a vic-
tim to it: and he told Hamlet of the envenomed point, and
said that Hamlet had not half an hour to live, for no medicine could cure him; and begging forgiveness of Hamlet,
he died, with his last words accusing the king of being the
contriver of the mischief. When Hamlet saw his end draw
near, there being yet some venom left upon the sword, he
suddenly turned upon his false uncle, and thrust the point
of it to his heart, fulfilling the promise which he had made
to his father's spirit, whose injunction was now accomplished, and his foul murder revenged upon the murderer.
Then Hamlet, feeling his breath fail and life departing,
turned to his dear friend Horatio, who had been spectator
of this fatal tragedy; and with his dying breath requested
him that he would live to tell his story to the world (for
Horatio had made a motion as if he would slay himself to
accompany the prince in death), and Horatio promised
that he would make a true report, as one that was privy to
all the circumstances. And, thus satisfied, the noble heart
of Hamlet cracked; and Horatio and the bystanders with
many tears commended the spirit of this sweet prince to
the guardianship of angels. For Hamlet was a loving and a
gentle prince, and greatly beloved for his many noble and
princelike qualities; and if he had lived, would no doubt
have proved a most royal and complete king to Denmark.

OTHELLO

Brabantio, the rich senator of Venice, had a fair daughter, the gentle Desdemona. She was sought to by divers suitors, both on account of her many virtuous qualities, and for her rich expectations. But among the suitors of her own clime and complexion, she saw none whom she could affect: for this noble lady, who regarded the mind more than the features of men, with a singularity rather to be admired than imitated, had chosen for the object of her affections, a Moor, a black, whom her father loved, and often invited to his house.

Neither is Desdemona to be altogether condemned for the unsuitableness of the person whom she selected for her lover. Bating that Othello was black, the noble Moor wanted nothing which might recommend him to the affections of the greatest lady. He was a soldier, and a brave one; and by his conduct in bloody wars against the Turks, had risen to the rank of general in the Venetian service, and was esteemed and trusted by the state.

He had been a traveller, and Desdemona (as is the manner of ladies) loved to hear him tell the story of his adventures, which he would run through from his earliest recollection; the battles, sieges, and encounters, which he had passed through; the perils he had been exposed to by land and by water; his hair-breadth escapes, when he had entered a breach, or marched up to the mouth of a cannon; and how he had been taken prisoner by the insolent enemy, and sold to slavery; how he demeaned himself in

that state, and how he escaped: all these accounts, added
to the narration of the strange things he had seen in foreign countries; the vast wilderness and romantic caverns,
the quarries, the rocks and mountains, whose heads are
in the clouds; of the savage nations, the cannibals who are
man-eaters, and a race of people in Africa whose heads do
grow beneath their shoulders: these travellers' stories
would so enchain the attention of Desdemona, that if she
were called off at any time by household affairs, she
would despatch with all haste that business, and return,
and with a greedy ear devour Othello's discourse. And
once he took advantage of a pliant hour, and drew from
her a prayer, that he would tell her the whole story of his
life at large, of which she had heard so much, but only by
parts: to which he consented, and beguiled her of many a
tear, when he spoke of some distressful stroke which his
youth had suffered.

His story being done, she gave him for his pains a world
of sighs: she swore a pretty oath, that it was all passing
strange, and pitiful, wondrous pitiful: she wished (she
said) she had not heard it, yet she wished that heaven had
made her such a man; and then she thanked him, and told
him, if he had a friend who loved her, he had only to teach
him how to tell his story, and that would woo her. Upon
this hint, delivered not with more frankness than modesty, accompanied with certain bewitching prettiness,
and blushes, which Othello could not but understand, he
spoke more openly of his love, and in this golden opportunity gained the consent of the generous lady Desdemona privately to marry him.

Neither Othello's colour nor his fortune were such that
it could be hoped Brabantio would accept him for a son-
in-law. He had left his daughter free; but he did expect
that, as the manner of noble Venetian ladies was, she
would choose ere long a husband of senatorial rank or
expectations; but in this he was deceived; Desdemona
loved the Moor, though he was black, and devoted her
heart and fortunes to his valiant parts and qualities; so

was her heart subdued to an implicit devotion to the man she had selected for a husband, that his very colour, which to all but this discerning lady would have proved an insurmountable objection, was by her esteemed above all the white skins and clear complexions of the young Venetian nobility, her suitors.

Their marriage, which, though privately carried, could not long be kept a secret, came to the ears of the old man, Brabantio, who appeared in a solemn council of the senate, as an accuser of the Moor Othello, who by spells and witchcraft (he maintained) had seduced the affections of the fair Desdemona to marry him, without the consent of her father, and against the obligations of hospitality.

At this juncture of time it happened that the state of Venice had immediate need of the services of Othello, news having arrived that the Turks with mighty preparation had fitted out a fleet, which was bending its course to the island of Cyprus, with intent to regain that strong post from the Venetians, who then held it; in this emergency the state turned its eyes upon Othello, who alone was deemed adequate to conduct the defence of Cyprus against the Turks. So that Othello, now summoned before the senate, stood in their presence at once as a candidate for a great state employment, and as a culprit, charged with offences which by the laws of Venice were made capital.

The age and senatorial character of old Brabantio, commanded a most patient hearing from that grave assembly; but the incensed father conducted his accusation with so much intemperance, producing likelihoods and allegations for proofs, that, when Othello was called upon for his defence, he had only to relate a plain tale of the course of his love; which he did with such an artless eloquence, recounting the whole story of his wooing, as we have related it above, and delivered his speech with so noble a plainness (the evidence of truth), that the duke, who sat as chief judge, could not help confessing that a tale so told would have won his daughter too: and the spells and conjurations which Othello had used in his courtship,

plainly appeared to have been no more than the honest
arts of men in love; and the only witchcraft which he had
used, the faculty of telling a soft tale to win a lady's ear.

This statement of Othello was confirmed by the testimony of the lady Desdemona herself, who appeared in
court, and professing a duty to her father for life and education, challenged leave of him to profess a yet higher
duty to her lord and husband, even so much as her
mother had shown in preferring him (Brabantio) above
her father.

The old senator, unable to maintain his plea, called the
Moor to him with many expressions of sorrow, and, as an
act of necessity, bestowed upon him his daughter, whom,
if he had been free to withhold her (he told him), he
would with all his heart have kept from him; adding, that
he was glad at soul that he had no other child, for this
behaviour of Desdemona would have taught him to be a
tyrant, and hang clogs on them for her desertion.

This difficulty being got over, Othello, to whom custom
had rendered the hardships of a military life as natural as
food and rest are to other men, readily undertook the
management of the wars in Cyprus: and Desdemona, preferring the honour of her lord (though with danger)
before the indulgence of those idle delights in which new-
married people usually waste their time, cheerfully consented to his going.

No sooner were Othello and his lady landed in Cyprus,
than news arrived, that a desperate tempest had dispersed
the Turkish fleet, and thus the island was secure from any
immediate apprehension of an attack. But the war, which
Othello was to suffer, was now beginning; and the enemies,
which malice stirred up against his innocent lady, proved in
their nature more deadly than strangers or infidels.

Among all the general's friends no one possessed the
confidence of Othello more entirely than Cassio. Michael
Cassio was a young soldier, a Florentine, gay, amorous,
and of pleasing address, favourite qualities with women;
he was handsome and eloquent, and exactly such a

person as might alarm the jealousy of a man advanced in years (as Othello in some measure was), who had married a young and beautiful wife; but Othello was as free from jealousy as he was noble, and as incapable of suspecting as of doing a base action. He had employed this Cassio in his love affair with Desdemona, and Cassio had been a sort of go-between in his suit: for Othello, fearing that himself had not those soft parts of conversation which please ladies, and finding these qualities in his friend, would often depute Cassio to go (as he phrased it) a courting for him: such innocent simplicity being rather an honour than a blemish to the character of the valiant Moor. So that no wonder, if next to Othello himself (but at far distance, as beseems a virtuous wife) the gentle Desdemona loved and trusted Cassio. Nor had the marriage of this couple made any difference in their behaviour to Michael Cassio. He frequented their house, and his free and rattling talk was no unpleasing variety to Othello, who was himself of a more serious temper: for such tempers are observed often to delight in their contraries, as a relief from the oppressive excess of their own: and Desdemona and Cassio would talk and laugh together, as in the days when he went a courting for his friend.

Othello had lately promoted Cassio to be the lieutenant, a place of trust, and nearest to the general's person. This promotion gave great offence to Iago, an older officer who thought he had a better claim than Cassio, and would often ridicule Cassio as a fellow fit only for the company of ladies, and one that knew no more of the art of war or how to set an army in array for battle, than a girl. Iago hated Cassio, and he hated Othello, as well for favouring Cassio, as for an unjust suspicion, which he had lightly taken up against Othello, that the Moor was too fond of Iago's wife Emilia. From these imaginary provocations, the plotting mind of Iago conceived a horrid scheme of revenge, which should involve both Cassio, the Moor, and Desdemona, in one common ruin.

Iago was artful, and had studied human nature deeply,

and he knew that of all the torments which afflict the mind of man (and far beyond bodily torture), the pains of jealousy were the most intolerable, and had the sorest sting. If he could succeed in making Othello jealous of Cassio, he thought it would be an exquisite plot of revenge, and might end in the death of Cassio or Othello, or both; he cared not.

The arrival of the general and his lady, in Cyprus, meeting with the news of the dispersion of the enemy's fleet, made a sort of holiday in the island. Everybody gave themselves up to feasting and making merry. Wine flowed in abundance, and cups went round to the health of the black Othello, and his lady the fair Desdemona.

Cassio had the direction of the guard that night, with a charge from Othello to keep the soldier from excess in drinking, that no brawl might arise, to fright the inhabitants, or disgust them with the new-landed forces. That night Iago began his deep-laid plans of mischief: under colour of loyalty and love to the general, he enticed Cassio to make rather too free with the bottle (a great fault in an officer upon guard). Cassio for a time resisted, but he could not long hold out against the honest freedom which Iago knew how to put on, but kept swallowing glass after glass (as Iago still plied him with drink and encouraging songs), and Cassio's tongue ran over in praise of the lady Desdemona, whom he again and again toasted, affirming that she was a most exquisite lady: until at last the enemy which he put into his mouth stole away his brains; and upon some provocation given him by a fellow whom Iago had set on, swords were drawn, and Montano, a worthy officer, who interfered to appease the dispute, was wounded in the scuffle. The riot now began to be general, and Iago, who had set on foot the mischief, was foremost in spreading the alarm, causing the castle-bell to be rung (as if some dangerous mutiny instead of a slight drunken quarrel had arisen): the alarm-bell ringing awakened Othello, who, dressing in a hurry, and coming to the scene of action, questioned Cassio of the cause. Cassio was now come to himself, the effect of the wine having a little gone off, but was too much ashamed to reply; and Iago, pretending a great reluctance to accuse Cassio, but, as it were, forced into it by Othello, who insisted to know the truth, gave an account of the whole matter (leaving out his own share in it, which Cassio was too far gone to remember) in such a manner, as while he seemed to make Cassio's offence less, did indeed make it appear greater than it was. The result was, that Othello, who was a strict observer of discipline, was compelled to take away Cassio's place of lieutenant from him.

Thus did Iago's first artifice succeed completely; he had now undermined his hated rival, and thrust him out of his place: but a further use was hereafter to be made of the adventure of this disastrous night.

Cassio, whom this misfortune had entirely sobered, now lamented to his seeming friend Iago that he should have been such a fool as to transform himself into a beast. He was undone, for how could he ask the general for his place again? he would tell him he was a drunkard. He despised himself. Iago, affecting to make light of it, said, that he, or any man living, might be drunk upon occasion; it remained now to make the best of a bad bargain; the general's wife was now the general, and could do anything with Othello; that he were best to apply to the lady Desdemona to mediate for him with her lord; that she was of a frank, obliging disposition, and would readily undertake a good office of this sort, and set Cassio right again in the general's favour; and then this crack in their love would be made stronger than ever. A good advice of Iago, if it had not been given for wicked purposes, which will after appear.

Cassio did as Iago advised him, and made application to the lady Desdemona, who was easy to be won over in any honest suit; and she promised Cassio that she should be his solicitor with her lord, and rather die than give up his cause. This she immediately set about in so earnest and pretty a manner, that Othello, who was mortally offended with Cassio, could not put her off. When he pleaded delay, and that it was too soon to pardon such an offender, she would not be beat back, but insisted that it should be the next night, or the morning after, or the next morning to that at farthest. Then she showed how penitent and humbled poor Cassio was, and that his offence did not deserve so sharp a check. And when Othello still hung back: 'What! my lord,' said she, 'that I should have so much to do to plead for Cassio, Michael Cassio, that came a courting for you, and oftentimes, when I have spoken in dispraise of you, has taken your part! I count this but a little thing to ask of you. When I mean to try your love indeed, I shall ask a weighty matter.' Othello could deny nothing to such a pleader, and only requesting that Desdemona would leave the time to him, promised to receive Michael Cassio again in favour.

It happened that Othello and Iago had entered into the room where Desdemona was, just as Cassio, who had been imploring her intercession, was departing at the opposite door: and Iago, who was full of art, said in a low voice, as if to himself: 'I like not that.' Othello took no great notice of what he said; indeed, the conference which immediately took place with his lady put it out of his head; but he remembered it afterwards. For when Desdemona was gone, Iago, as if for mere satisfaction of his thought, questioned Othello whether Michael Cassio, when Othello was courting his lady, knew of his love. To this the general answering in the affirmative and adding, that he had gone between them very often during the courtship, Iago knitted his brow, as if he had got fresh light on some terrible matter, and cried: 'Indeed!' This brought into Othello's mind the words which Iago had let fall upon entering the room, and seeing Cassio with Desdemona; and he began to think there was some meaning in all this: for he deemed Iago to be a just man, and full of love and honesty, and what in a false knave would be tricks, in him seemed to be the natural workings of an honest mind, big with something too great for utterance:

and Othello prayed Iago to speak what he knew, and to give his worst thoughts words. 'And what,' said Iago, 'if some thoughts very vile should have intruded into my breast, as where is the palace into which foul things do not enter?' Then Iago went on to say, what a pity it were, if any trouble should arise to Othello out of his imperfect observations; that it would not be for Othello's peace to know his thoughts; that people's good names were not to be taken away for slight suspicions; and when Othello's curiosity was raised almost to distraction with these hints and scattered words, Iago, as if in earnest care for Othello's peace of mind, besought him to beware of jealousy: with such art did this villain raise suspicions in the unguarded Othello, by the very caution which he pretended to give him against suspicion. 'I know,' said Othello, 'that my wife is fair, loves company and feasting, is free of speech, sings, plays, and dances well: but where virtue is, these qualities are virtuous. I must have proof before I think her dishonest.' Then Iago, as if glad that Othello was slow to believe ill of his lady, frankly declared that he had no proof, but begged Othello to observe her behaviour well, when Cassio was by; not to be jealous nor too secure neither, for that he (Iago) knew the dispositions of the Italian ladies, his countrywomen, better than Othello could do; and that in Venice the wives let heaven see many pranks they dared not show their husbands. Then he artfully insinuated that Desdemona deceived her father in marrying with Othello, and carried it so closely, that the poor old man thought that witchcraft had been used. Othello was much moved with this argument, which brought the matter home to him, for if she had deceived her father, why might she not deceive her husband?

Iago begged pardon for having moved him; but Othello, assuming an indifference, while he was really shaken with inward grief at Iago's words, begged him to go on, which Iago did with many apologies, as if unwilling to produce anything against Cassio, whom he called his friend: he then came strongly to the point, and reminded Othello

how Desdemona had refused many suitable matches of
her own clime and complexion, and had married him, a
Moor, which showed unnatural in her, and proved her to
have a headstrong will; and when her better judgement
returned, how probable it was she should fall upon comparing Othello with the fine forms and clear white complexions of the young Italians her countrymen. He concluded with advising Othello to put off his reconcilement
with Cassio a little longer, and in the meanwhile to note
with what earnestness Desdemona should intercede in
his behalf; for that much would be seen in that. So mis-
chievously did this artful villain lay his plots to turn the
gentle qualities of this innocent lady into her destruction,
and make a net for her out of her own goodness to entrap
her: first setting Cassio on to entreat her mediation, and
then out of that very mediation contriving stratagems for
her ruin.

The conference ended with Iago's begging Othello to
account his wife innocent, until he had more decisive
proof; and Othello promised to be patient; but from that
moment the deceived Othello never tasted content of
mind. Poppy, nor the juice of mandragora, nor all the
sleeping potions in the world, could ever again restore to
him that sweet rest, which he had enjoyed but yesterday.
His occupation sickened upon him. He no longer took
delight in arms. His heart, that used to be roused at the
sight of troops, and banners, and battle-array, and would
stir and leap at the sound of a drum, or a trumpet, or a
neighing war-horse, seemed to have lost all that pride and
ambition which are a soldier's virtue; and his military
ardour and all his old joys forsook him. Sometimes he
thought his wife honest, and at times he thought her not
so; sometimes he thought Iago just, and at times he
thought him not so; then he would wish that he had never
known of it; he was not the worse for her loving Cassio, so
long as he knew it not: torn to pieces with these distract-
ing thoughts, he once laid hold on Iago's throat, and
demanded proof of Desdemona's guilt, or threatened

instant death for his having belied her. Iago, feigning
indignation that his honesty should be taken for a vice,
asked Othello, if he had not sometimes seen a handkerchief spotted with strawberries in his wife's hand. Othello
answered, that he had given her such a one, and that it
was his first gift. 'That same handkerchief,' said Iago, 'did
I see Michael Cassio this day wipe his face with.' 'If it be
as you say,' said Othello, 'I will not rest till a wide revenge
swallow them up: and first, for a token of your fidelity, I
expect that Cassio shall be put to death within three days;
and for that fair devil (meaning his lady), I will withdraw
and devise some swift means of death for her.'

Trifles light as air are to the jealous proofs as strong as
holy writ. A handkerchief of his wife's seen in Cassio's
hand, was motive enough to the deluded Othello to pass
sentence of death upon them both, without once inquiring how Cassio came by it. Desdemona had never given
such a present to Cassio, nor would this constant lady
have wronged her lord with doing so naughty a thing
as giving his presents to another man; both Cassio and
Desdemona were innocent of any offence against Othello:
but the wicked Iago, whose spirits never slept in contrivance of villany, had made his wife (a good, but a weak
woman) steal this handkerchief from Desdemona, under
pretence of getting the work copied, but in reality to drop
it in Cassio's way, where he might find it, and give a handle to Iago's suggestion that it was Desdemona's present.

Othello, soon after meeting his wife, pretended that he
had a headache (as he might indeed with truth), and
desired her to lend him her handkerchief to hold to his
temples. She did so. 'Not this,' said Othello, 'but that
handkerchief I gave you.' Desdemona had it not about her
(for indeed it was stolen, as we have related). 'How?' said
Othello, 'this is a fault indeed. That handkerchief an
Egyptian woman gave to my mother; the woman was a
witch and could read people's thoughts: she told my
mother, while she kept it, it would make her amiable, and
my father would love her; but, if she lost it, or gave it

away, my father's fancy would turn, and he would loathe her as much as he had loved her. She dying gave it to me, and bade me, if I ever married, to give it to my wife. I did so; take heed of it. Make it a darling as precious as your eye.' 'It is possible?' said the frighted lady. ' 'Tis true,' continued Othello; 'it is a magical handkerchief; a sibyl that had lived in the world two hundred years, in a fit of prophetic fury worked it; the silkworms that furnished the silk were hallowed, and it was dyed in a mummy of maidens' hearts conserved.' Desdemona, hearing the wondrous virtues of the handkerchief, was ready to die with fear, for she plainly perceived she had lost it, and with it, she feared, the affections of her husband. Then Othello started, and looked as if he were going to do some rash thing, and still he demanded the handkerchief, which when she could not produce, she tried to divert her husband from too serious thoughts, and cheerfully told him she saw all his talk about the handkerchief was only to put her off from her suit about Michael Cassio, whom she went on to praise (as Iago had foretold), till Othello in perfect distraction burst out of the room, and then Desdemona, though unwillingly, began to suspect that her lord was jealous.

What cause she could have ministered to him she knew not, and then she accused herself for accusing the noble Othello, and thought to be sure that some untoward news from Venice, or some state troubles had muddled his spirits, and made his temper not so sweet as formerly. And she said: 'Men are not gods, and we must not look for that observance from them when they are married, which they show us on the bridal day.' And she beshrewed herself for so unkindly judging of his unkindness.

Again Othello and Desdemona met, and he accused her more plainly of being unfaithful, and of loving another man, but he did not name whom: and Othello wept, and Desdemona said: 'Alas! the heavy day! why do you weep?' And Othello told her, he could have borne all sorts of evils with fortitude—poverty, and disease, and disgrace; but her infidelity had broken his heart: and he called her a weed, that looked so fair, and smelled so sweet, that the sense ached at it; and wished she had never been born. And when he had left her, this innocent lady was so stupefied with wonder at her lord's untrue suspicion of her, that a weight-like sleep came over her, and she only desired her attendant to make her bed, and to lay her wedding-sheets upon it, saying, that when people teach their babes, they do it by gentle means and easy tasks, and Othello might have chid her so; for in good faith she was but a child when she was chidden. And this was all the complaint which this gentle lady made.

Desdemona being retired to bed expecting her lord would follow her, soon fell into a slumber, the effect of her troubled spirits, when Othello entered the chamber, full of the black purpose which he had meditated of putting his lady to death. But when he saw her asleep, he thought he would not shed her blood, nor scar that white skin of hers, more white than alabaster. But he was resolved she should die; else (as he said) she would live to betray more men, as she had done him. Then he kissed her for the last time (as he said), and that kiss was so sweet, that he must needs kiss her again: and he wept, but he said they were cruel tears.

Desdemona was awakened with his kisses, and she looked upon Othello, and she saw him gnaw his under lip, and roll his eyes, and she knew he was always fatal when he looked so: and he bade her prepare for death, and to say her prayers, for he would not kill her soul. And this innocent wife, as she lay at his mercy, begged for compassion, and to know her fault, and then he named Cassio, and the handkerchief which (he said) she had given him; and as the guiltless lady was proceeding to clear herself he suddenly would hear no more, but covering her up in the bed-clothes, stifled her till she died.

In this instant of time was brought into the house Cassio, wounded and bleeding, whom Iago had set one of his creatures on to assassinate; but the fellow not succeeding in his attempt to kill Cassio (whom he wounded, but not mortally), and being himself killed by Iago to prevent discovery, in his pockets were found certain letters, which made the guilt of Iago, and the innocence of Cassio, clear beyond all doubt; and Cassio now came to beg pardon of Othello, and to ask wherein he had offended him, that he had employed Iago to murder him.

This discovery was as a thunderstroke to Othello, who now plainly saw that he was no better than a murderer, and that his wife (poor innocent lady) had been ever faithful to him; the extreme anguish of which discovery making life insupportable, he fell upon his sword, and throwing himself upon the body of his dear injured lady, expired.

These rash acts raised much passion of horror and amazement in the bystanders, for Othello had borne a fair reputation, and till he was wrought upon by the arts of a villain, which his own noble nature never gave him leave to suspect, he was a loving and a doting husband. He had loved not wisely, but too well; and his manly eyes (when he learned his mistake), though not used to weep on every small occasion, dropped tears as fast as the Arabian trees their gum. And when he was dead all his former merits and his valiant acts were remembered. Nothing now remained for his successor but to put the utmost censure of the law in force against Iago, who was executed with strict tortures; and to send word to the state of Venice of the lamentable death of their renowned general.

DOVER EVERGREEN CLASSICS